There's something in the bushes. . . .

Barbara stopped. Had she heard something?

There it was again, coming from inside the boxwood hedges. A coughing sound.

Barbara looked at the thick, green bushes but could see nothing. "Who is that?" she asked. "Rodney, are you spying on me? You best leave me alone!"

There was no answer. Barbara crossed her arms and demanded, "Who is there?"

Still no answer. *I'm just imagining it,* she told herself. *I'll bet it was only a rabbit or a kitten rustling the leaves.* She parted the woody branches of the hedges with her fingers and put her face to the leaves, trying to see. "Kitty, kitty, kitty," she said. The shadows within the brush were very dark.

"Kitty, kitty, kitty." She pushed her face even closer.

And then she stumbled backward with a scream.

There had been eyes in the bushes, just an inch away from her own. Wide, staring, *human* eyes!

**Books in the DAUGHTERS OF LIBERTY series
(by Elizabeth Massie)**

Patsy's Discovery
Patsy and the Declaration
Barbara's Escape

Available from MINSTREL Books

DAUGHTERS *of* LIBERTY

BARBARA'S ESCAPE

Elizabeth Massie

A
MINSTREL®
BOOK

Published by POCKET BOOKS
New York   London   Toronto   Sydney   Tokyo   Singapore

This book is a work of fiction. Names, characters, places and incidents are products of the author's imagination or are used fictiously. Any resemblance to actual events or locales or persons, living or dead, is entirely coincidental.

A MINSTREL PAPERBACK *Original*

A Minstrel Book published by
POCKET BOOKS, a division of Simon & Schuster Inc.
1230 Avenue of the Americas, New York, NY 10020

ISBN: 0-671-00134-5

First Minstrel Books printing September 1997

10 9 8 7 6 5 4 3 2 1

A MINSTREL BOOK and colophon are registered trademarks of Simon & Schuster Inc.

Cover art by Ernie Norcia

Printed in the U.S.A.

To Ananda Wimberger, with all best wishes for love, peace, wonder, and bliss. Give your parents a hug for me!

1

"Little Bit!" Barbara Layman scolded. "You hold still now!"

The dapple gray pony stomped her front feet and shook her head, sending soapy water in a mad spray all over Barbara and the paddock fence.

"Gracious," said Barbara. The thirteen-year-old wiped soap bubbles from her nose and dropped the washrag into the bucket at her feet. Her mob-cap had slid sideways on her head, and strands of curly black hair had fallen free of the pins. Her skirt and apron were wet, and her leather shoes were caked in mud. She knew she was a mess, but at that moment she couldn't be bothered. She had a pony to wash. "That was not nice. I'm trying to make you beautiful like a real lady and all you want to do is struggle."

The pony turned her head and nudged Barbara's shoulder with her velvety nose.

"Are you trying to make up with me?"

The pony's head went up and down, as if she were nodding.

"Fine, then," said Barbara. She pushed the sleeves of her pink linen dress past her elbows and wrung out the rag. "Now, just a few more minutes and you'll be so clean Mother will let you come upstairs and have dinner with us tonight."

Little Bit shook her head back and forth.

"No?" Barbara giggled. "I suppose you're right. I guess you'll have to be content to eat in your stall. But a fine dinner of hay I'll give you. Fine hay and tasty water, fresh and cold from the well, and some grain. You'll feel like a true lady, my dear."

It was mid-afternoon on July 7th. Barbara had been given some free time until dinner, at four o'clock. She had decided that her pony was due for a bath, even though her father thought it was a waste of time.

"Goodness, girl," he'd said when he saw her lugging a bucket and sliver of lye soap to the paddock.

"Why are you bothering to clean that animal? She'll only roll in the dust again and your time will have been wasted."

Barbara had answered honestly, "She rolled in manure yesterday. I don't care to ride her and then be accused of rolling in manure myself!"

Barbara's father had laughed in agreement. He was a tall, cheerful man with thinning hair pulled back at the nape of his neck. Unlike some other men in Philadelphia, he never wore a wig—he had no use for them. "Wigs are a waste of money," he would say. "And we are not fancy people. With my work, I need a simple man's garb."

Mr. Layman was the stable manager at Black's Tavern, a popular establishment on Mulberry Street for boarding gentlemen and their horses. Barbara, her mother, and father lived in the two rooms above the stable. Even though Barbara had many chores in the stable and in the family's vegetable garden, she enjoyed her life. She was able to spend time with animals and be outdoors in the fresh air often. She was also able to do many fun things that her best friend, Patsy Black, daughter of the tavern's owner, was not allowed to do because they weren't considered "ladylike."

Barbara finished the pony with a good rinse of

clear, cold water from a second bucket. Next, she shoved her hair back beneath her cap and rinsed her hands off in the paddock trough. At last, she attached a lead line to the pony's halter and took her through the paddock gate to the alley behind the stable.

Mr. Layman, who was cleaning a saddle in the tack room, called from the open window, "Where are you off to, Barbara?"

"I want to let Little Bit dry off. If I let her loose now, she'll only roll again, and wet, she'll not only smell of manure, she'll be covered in it."

"Don't be long," Mr. Layman answered. "There are stalls that need mucking."

Barbara and Little Bit took the alley out to Philadelphia's busy Mulberry Street. The sun was high in the sky and there was not a cloud to be seen. The men and women who strolled along the street or bounced along in their carriages and wagons seemed tired from the oppressive heat. There was little chatter to be heard. Shaded areas under trees at the side of the road had become popular places; boys gathered there to study and exchange marbles, women clustered about in the shadows to fan themselves. Even oily-feathered starlings preferred to peck at the ground beneath the trees rather than be out in the glaring sunlight.

Little Bit slowed and tried to lower her nose to a patch of grass poking through the gravel of the road. "Come on," said Barbara, tugging the rope lead. "I told Father we were out to dry you off, and that is true. But I also have somewhere to go. The silversmith, Mr. Ford, has a new mare and foal, and I want to see them. Father said they were quite a handsome pair."

Down the road went Barbara and her reluctant pony. They passed a bookbinder's, a printer's shop, a tailor's shop, and the home of the music teacher, Mistress Marks. From the parlor window of Mistress Marks's home, Barbara could hear someone pounding painfully at the keys of a harpsichord and the muffled voice of the frustrated teacher.

"Not so hard, Miss Roseman! You are a lady and should play like a lady. It sounds as if a mad cat were racing up and down the keys. Now, let's try again." The keys were struck again, bringing forth a glaring, inharmonious chord. Little Bit's ears went flat and the pony shivered. Mistress Marks wailed with impatience. Giggling, Barbara walked on.

"Hello, Barbara Layman!" called a girl from the

side of the street. Coming out of the baker's shop were Abby Boxler and her mother. Abby was Barbara's age, with straight dark hair and brown eyes. Her mother owned Boxler's Milliner, where hats and fabric and fine dresses were sold. Abby wore a deep blue dress with a white shawl and apron. On her head was a blue-ribbon–trimmed bonnet. "How nice to see you. Are you taking your pony to the marketplace? Is she for sale?" Abby asked.

Barbara shook her head. "Oh, no. I'm only taking her on a stroll until she dries off."

Abby came out to the street. Beneath her arm was a box that smelled of a freshly baked cake. "Why must you walk her?" Abby asked. "She would dry off quite naturally in her paddock."

"You don't know my pony," Barbara answered. "She would roll as soon as I let go of her halter, caking herself with mud and worse. It's best I keep her moving."

Mrs. Boxler walked over to the girls. She was a happy, plump woman with bright red hair. Her dress was purple satin, with sleeves and collar trimmed in tatted lace and black velvet ribbon. "Hello, Barbara. So nice to see you. But I'm afraid we can't stay and chat. We must get back to the shop."

"Are you having a party?" Barbara asked, nodding at the cake box.

"No," said Abby. "Mother did an alteration on one of the baker's gowns. But she has paid us in goods instead of money. It is a wonderful cake. I can't wait to taste it."

Barbara knew that times were hard for many of the merchants in Philadelphia. Colonists from New England to Pennsylvania to Virginia were fighting against the soldiers of England because the King of England had refused to give the colonists the freedoms they deserved. Although Barbara had seen no battles in the city yet, the citizens were affected in many ways. Some shop owners had lost their businesses because the ships carrying the goods they imported from Europe were stopped by British forces. Mrs. Boxler's hat and clothing shop was failing because she could no longer get fancy fabrics from Europe. Other Philadelphia merchants, who depended on the income of the importers to help support their own shops, were likewise suffering.

"Before we must go," Abby said, "quickly show us one of Little Bit's tricks."

"Which one?" asked Barbara. "I've taught her quite a few."

"A new trick, then."

Barbara centered herself in front of Little Bit and held her hand up. "Little Bit," she said. "I see a gentleman. Where are your manners?" She then gently tapped the pony between her ears. Little Bit tucked her right front leg back and bowed.

"That's wonderful!" said Abby.

"She's very smart," said Mrs. Boxler. Laughing, the woman curtsied to the pony. "I bid you farewell, Miss Little Bit! And, Barbara, please give your mother my best." She and Abby departed, and Barbara once again guided the pony down Mulberry Street.

Earl Ford's silversmith shop was a two-story brick building on Third Street. It had red shutters and a whitewashed picket fence. A wooden sign reading E. Ford hung over the front door. Painted beneath the letters were a platter, cream pitcher, and marrow spoon. Many shop signs showed pictures instead of words. This way, even someone who couldn't read would know what type of business it was.

At the roadside in front of the shop was a post for horses. Barbara tied Little Bit's rope lead securely and yanked on it to make sure it would hold. She patted Little Bit on the neck, happy to see that in the summer heat, the pony was nearly dry.

"Hello!" Barbara called as she entered the shop. Although small, the place was bright and sparkly with freshly polished silver. New candlesticks, plates, and bowls lined the windows and the shelves. Mr. Ford, one of the finest craftsmen in Philadelphia, attracted the richest people in the city to his shop. Barbara's family, who worked and lived at Black's Tavern stable, couldn't afford such luxuries. Admiring its mirrorlike shine, Barbara touched a bright tea set on a small table near the door.

"Good afternoon. May I help you?" A boy came out of the back room, wiping his hands on a stiff, white apron. He wore streaks of tarnish on his arms and a frown on his face.

"Good afternoon," said Barbara. "My name is Barbara Layman. My father told me that Mr. Ford has a new mare and foal. I was hoping I could see them."

The boy pursed his lips. "Mr. Ford is busy working. I don't think he would have time to show you his animals. Now, run along."

"Who are you?"

"Mr. Ford's new apprentice. Now, be off unless you have a purchase to make."

Barbara frowned. She would not let this boy talk to her in such a manner, nor throw her out. "Mr. Ford said I could come by anytime to see them. Tell him I've come by."

But the boy frowned and put his hands on his hips. "Little girl, unless you've got business here, you are wasting my time. Now, if you will just . . ."

Mr. Ford came into the front room. He was a man in his fifties, with hair as silver as the fine crafts he created. He was a kind, cheerful man, and had been boyhood friends with Barbara's father many years ago in Virginia. The two had lost track of each other when the Fords had moved north. But when Mr. Layman had brought his family to Philadelphia three years ago, the men had run into each other in the Market Place on High Street. They got together on occasion to talk about old times and swap stories.

"Good afternoon, Miss Layman," Mr. Ford said. He smiled and bowed in a gentlemanly manner, one foot before the other, one hand behind his back. "How very fine to see you. Rodney, why didn't you tell me Miss Layman was here?"

"Sir, she is being a nuisance," said Rodney. "She

doesn't intend to buy anything. She merely wants to see your new horses!"

"So," said Mr. Ford, "why didn't you come and tell me? You are my apprentice, Rodney, not my partner. You don't make decisions here, I do."

Rodney scowled at Barbara, but said, "Yes, sir."

Mr. Ford's voice was stern. "Go back and finish polishing the new pieces. I expect them to be perfect, not a smudge nor a fingerprint. Your father and mother sent you here to learn a trade from me, and I will do all I can to see that you do. But you must follow my orders without question. Only this way can you someday become a true master of the craft."

"Yes, sir." Rodney sighed heavily and left the room.

Mr. Ford watched Rodney as the boy left, but then turned and chuckled softly. "So," he said to Barbara. "You came to see my mare and foal?"

Barbara nodded. "Yes, sir. Would you show me where they are, if it's not inconvenient?"

"I will be happy to," Mr. Ford said. "They are both prizes, they are. Fine animals and as healthy as any I've seen. I got them in the market several weeks ago from a farmer from Maryland. I haven't got time to take you out back, but you know your way around horses, so I shall let you visit them on your own. Just make sure you latch the gate securely as you leave."

"Oh, yes, sir!" said Barbara.

Mr. Ford pulled something out of his pocket and pressed it into Barbara's palm. "Give the mare this. I know I shouldn't, but on occasion it should be all right, don't you think?" It was a cube of sugar.

"Thank you," said Barbara. She pulled the shop door open. "Oh, and what are their names?"

"I haven't decided. Perhaps you can give me suggestions later?"

"Oh, yes, sir," said Barbara, nodding enthusiastically. "That would be fun." She skipped outside.

The small barn was in the shop's backyard, set apart from the rest of the lawn by a rail fence. Barbara took the brick walkway through thick boxwood hedges to the fence gate. She unlatched it and went into the barnyard. As she approached, several of Mr. Ford's hens squawked and ran behind a grain barrel. Tiny yellow chicks followed their mothers into the shadows.

Along the far wall were four stalls for horses. The bottom part of the stall doors were closed; the tops were open. Barbara peered into the first stall.

It was empty. She moved to the second stall and stood on tiptoe to have a look.

Inside stood a sleek, golden mare with a creamy white mane and tail. Lying on the straw beside her was a black foal, his nose tucked between his front legs, his soft little tail swishing back and forth.

"Gracious sakes!" Barbara said. "You both are beautiful."

The mare's ears pricked up and she stepped to the door. Barbara took the sugar cube from her pocket and held it out on her palm. The horse took it and, with a single crunch, swallowed it. She sniffed Barbara's hand for more.

"There was only one," said Barbara. "Sorry."

With slow, awkward movements, the foal got his wobbly legs beneath him and stumbled to the door. Barbara stood on tiptoes and stretched her arm out, catching the foal's soft neck with her fingers. "You, I would name you Dark Star," she said to the baby. "And you," she said to the mother, "you, pretty girl, I would name Sun Star."

The foal whinnied softly and the mare nuzzled his neck. Barbara gazed at the two, thinking how much fun it would be to watch them race side by side in a broad, green field. Maybe when Dark Star was older, Mr. Ford would let Barbara spend time training him. She had trained Little Bit and knew about horses' moods and temperaments. She liked horses, and horses seemed to like her, too.

From out on the street, Barbara heard her own pony nickering. "I've left Little Bit for longer than she'd like," she told the mare and foal. "I do believe she's either lonely or jealous. Good-bye, and I hope to see you again."

Barbara left the barnyard, latched the gate, and strolled up the brick walk between the hedges. A squirrel fussed at her from the branches of a maple tree. From the top of a bird bottle on the house next door, a blue jay shrieked at her. And a little brown vole scampered up the walk and darted beneath the gate.

"Dark Star and Sun Star," Barbara said to herself, trying the names out again on the air. "I think they suit. I'm sure Mr. Ford will like them."

And then the sound of coughing, coming from inside the boxwood hedges, startled Barbara.

She stopped and looked at the thick, green bushes but could see nothing. "Who is that?" she asked. "Rodney, are you spying on me? Mr. Ford said I could see the horses, so you best leave me alone!"

There was no answer. Barbara crossed her arms and demanded, "Who is there?"

Still no answer. *I'm just imagining it,* she told herself. *I'll bet it was only a rabbit or a kitten rustling the leaves.* She parted the woody branches of the hedges with her fingers and put her face to the leaves, trying to see. "Kitty, kitty, kitty," she said. The shadows within the brush were very dark.

"Kitty, kitty, kitty." She pushed her face even closer.

And then she stumbled backward with a scream. She fell to the walkway and bounced. Her mobcap flopped to the side and hung by a single hairpin against her neck.

There had been eyes in the bushes, just an inch away from her own. Wide, staring, *human* eyes!

2

Mr. Ford was through the gate and racing down the walk in a second, running to Barbara.

"Are you all right?" he shouted, his white apron strings flapping. "What happened?"

Barbara sat on the bricks, staring at the bushes where she had seen the eyes. Her heart pounded wildly. Who was in there? Was it a burglar, coming to rob Mr. Ford of his precious wares? Was it a horse thief, coming to steal away the mare and the foal?

She pointed at the hedges with a trembling finger. "In there," she managed. "I saw someone hiding!"

Mr. Ford helped Barbara to her feet. She jerked

her mobcap off and clutched it in one hand. "Look, catch him before he's gone!"

Rodney rushed up, his face no longer full of the irritation Barbara had seen in the shop. This time, he seemed to be frightened. "What's the matter?" He twisted the edge of a polishing cloth in his hands.

"Stand back," said Mr. Ford, turning to the hedges. "Whoever is there, I demand that you come out, now."

There was no movement in the bushes. No sound.

"Come out, now," said Mr. Ford. He grabbed a handful of stubby branches and gave them a severe shake. "You are on my property without permission. You are trespassing. Would you not rather be ordered out for trespassing than arrested for attempted theft?"

Still there was no movement and no sound.

Mr. Ford waved his hand for Barbara and Rodney to move back even farther. He leaned into the brush and looked around. A moment later, he pulled his head back out. "There's nothing in there," he said. "There's no one."

"Are you certain?" asked Barbara. "I saw them, I saw the eyes."

"There is no one there now," said Mr. Ford.

Now, Rodney was brave again. He chuckled with annoyance and rolled his eyes. "She's a girl," he said. "She's got a girl's silly imagination."

Barbara whirled on the apprentice. "You know nothing of me, boy. I dare say if you'd seen the eyes in that hedge you'd have been running off in tears! Now you keep your opinion to yourself."

Rodney's jaw dropped. He sputtered for a moment and said, "You have no manners, little miss! What poor training you've had at home! A pity, to be certain."

"Pity is something you feel sorry for," said Barbara. "And I feel sorry that you know so little of girls."

"Enough," said Mr. Ford. "Rodney, back to work. Barbara, are you hurt from your fall?"

"No, sir," said Barbara. She peered at the hedges, certain she'd seen eyes staring at her. "I'm fine."

"I'm glad," said Mr. Ford. "Now, before I bid you good afternoon, tell me, did you think of a name for my new animals?"

"Yes, sir. If they were my horses, I would name the mare Sun Star and her foal Dark Star. They are a lovely pair, indeed."

Mr. Ford rubbed his chin and smiled. "I like the names, Barbara. I will give them serious consideration." With a bow, he strode back up the walkway to the shop.

Barbara watched him go, then looked at the boxwoods. "Someone's in there, I know it." She put her hands on her hips and shook her head. She stuck her mobcap in the pocket of her apron. Then she turned on her toes and went up the walk.

As she reached the fence at the side of the shop and touched the gate to open it, she heard the cough again.

She spun around.

But this time, she didn't scream. Instead, taking a deep, silent breath, she tiptoed back to the place where she'd heard the noise. *I'll be very quiet,* she thought. *I'll peek in to see who it is, then go tell Mr. Ford. After all, I'm a Daughter of Liberty. I am a spy!*

Slowly, Barbara leaned into the brush. She looked, but saw nothing. Then she heard the cough again, and this time it came from a cluster of holly trees by Mr. Ford's well house on the other side of the backyard. She squeezed between two hedges and crept across the small yard to the holly trees.

Who is there? In spite of her brave thoughts,

Barbara felt the backs of her hands grow cold with apprehension.

Careful not to scratch herself too badly on the spiny leaves, Barbara pushed the branches apart and looked into the trees.

A girl was huddled on the ground. She wore a plain blue dress and scarf on her head. It was hard to see her face because of the darkness under the trees. The girl crouched at the far side of the trees, her back against the well house. She stared at Barbara; Barbara stared at her.

"My goodness!" Barbara exclaimed. "Who are you?"

The girl said nothing. She tried to press herself farther away but couldn't move. The sharp-leaved trees, the tangle of branches, and the well house kept her in place.

"Why are you hiding?" asked Barbara.

The girl opened her mouth as though she was going to answer, but then she shut it again.

"Are you in trouble?"

The girl's hands, which were wrapped about her knees, drew up into fists.

I wonder if she's a British spy? Barbara thought. *If I've found one, I must not let on I know. Won't Patsy be excited when I tell her!*

"Can you come out?" asked Barbara. "I promise I won't tell Mr. Ford that you are here."

The girl ran one fist under her nose. She coughed, then sniffed. Barbara realized that the girl was crying.

"What's wrong? You can talk to me," said Barbara. "My name is Barbara Layman. I live over on Mulberry Street, at Black's Tavern. Are you lost?"

Very slowly, the girl nodded.

Barbara crawled beneath the trees and stopped several feet from the girl. Closer, she could see that the girl's dress was torn in several places. Her foot could be seen from beneath the hem of her skirt; it was bare. Her skin was black, nearly as dark as the shadows. "Don't you want to come out where we won't get scratched?" Barbara asked.

The girl shook her head.

Barbara held out her hand. "Come on. I can help you if you're lost. I know my way around Philadelphia. I've lived here for several years, and my parents allow me to do errands all over. Will you come out?"

The girl shook her head again.

"Barbara?" It was Mr. Ford. He'd come back out to the yard. The girl shivered at his voice and gave Barbara a look that asked, *Are you going to tell on me?* But Barbara shook her head to let the girl know she would say nothing.

"Where are you?" Mr. Ford continued. "Are you all right? Your pony is most troubled by your absence. I'm afraid she's dug a hole in the ground deep enough to bury the dead."

Barbara quickly crawled from beneath the trees, her stockings snagging on the ground and ripping a huge hole in the knee. Her hair caught on holly leaves and tangled into a knot. She hopped to her feet and saw Mr. Ford peering over the boxwood hedges.

"Hello, I'm fine," she said. "I saw a cat and thought she might be yours. But she ran off."

"A cat?" asked Mr. Ford. "I don't own a cat, although I should, I believe. It would help keep mice out of my barn."

"Well," Barbara said as she joined Mr. Ford on the walk, "one of our cats at Black's stable had kittens just three weeks ago. Would you like one when they are old enough to leave their mother?"

Mr. Ford rubbed his chin. "I would at that. Thank you."

They walked out to the street, where Barbara untied Little Bit from the post. Indeed, the pony had pawed a substantial pit in the road. Somehow she would have to train the animal not to do that. Barbara tossed the rope reins over her pony's neck. "Would you like two cats, perhaps?" she asked Mr. Ford as he pushed open his door to go into his shop. "Or three or four?"

Mr. Ford leaned back and laughed. "One will be fine, Barbara. But thank you for your generosity!"

Little Bit was dry now, and a thin coating of street dust lay on her dapple coat. Barbara tossed the lead rope over her pony's neck and tied it to the halter ring. She could ride back to Black's Tavern, even though young ladies weren't expected to ride a horse bareback, much less astraddle.

But she hesitated before mounting, looking back at Mr. Ford's side yard and the brick walk and the boxwoods.

Who is that girl? Why is she so frightened?

Little Bit tucked her nose under Barbara's arm and gave a shove. The pony was more than ready to go.

"All right," Barbara said. She hopped up, gathered the lead rope in her fingers, and tapped Little Bit's sides with her heels. And the two headed back along the street toward Black's Tavern.

3

Barbara grabbed her friend Patsy's sleeve and gave
it a tug. "We have to hurry. We don't want to miss
this! Would you just come on?"

"I'm coming, I'm coming," said twelve-year-old
Patsy Black as she dumped the pebble from her
leather shoe, waving one hand in the air in an at-
tempt to keep her balance. "Just give me a moment, please! My foot hurts."

Barbara let go of Patsy's sleeve and sighed as
the girl dropped the shoe to the road and slipped
it back on. Up ahead several yards were Patsy's
and Barbara's families. It was July 8, and they were
all on their way to Chestnut Street—Barbara's parents, Della and Paul Layman; Patsy's parents, Re-

becca and Andrew Black; Patsy's two brothers, sixteen-year-old Henry and seven-year-old Nicholas; and even Patsy's new baby sister, Dorcas. Mr. Black had left the care of the tavern in the hands of the cook, Katherine Ralston, and the two older Quaker ladies, the Anderson twins, who did assorted jobs about the tavern. It was rare that Mr. Black would allow everyone in the family to be away from the tavern at a given time, but everyone wanted to go to the State House to hear the declaration, which was going to be read publicly for the first time.

Barbara and Patsy raced to catch up with their families. "Whoa, there," said Mr. Black, turning to look at his daughter as she passed him. "You mustn't run, my girl. What will you look like with such a flushed face? A boy, I fear!"

Nicholas giggled and pointed at his sister. "Patsy looks like a boy! Patsy looks like a boy!"

Patsy made a face at Nicholas, then looked at Barbara and grimaced. Barbara covered her smile with her hand. *My father never says such things to me,* she thought. *I'm lucky for that.*

The families trudged south along Fifth Street, joining with others who were also going to the State House. Women chatted excitedly with each other; Quakers in their plain black garb moved along the walk in solemn procession. Men in wigs and tricornered hats talked as they proceeded down the street, some with raised and angry voices, about what had happened just several days earlier at the State House.

Barbara linked arms with Patsy as they strolled with their families. A man on horseback raced past, spraying the girls with dirt and small stones.

"Vexation," Patsy grumbled, slapping at the dust on her skirt. But Barbara didn't pay it any attention. There was too much on her mind.

A band of sailors of the new Navy marched across the street, heading east toward the river. They looked fine and strong in blue coats with red trim, brass buttons, black hats and shoes, and black leather sword scabbards. One man carried a yellow flag with a rattlesnake emblem. Barbara guessed that these men would muster on the Delaware and launch out to face the British Navy in some dreadful yet important battle. What brave men these were, because, indeed, the British Navy was the best and strongest in the world. Ever since the Americans had begun fighting in 1775, many people thought they could never defeat the British. Some thought it was mad to imagine a tiny collection of rough colonists could overcome such a powerful country as England.

We have been at war, Barbara thought. *But now, it is official.* Delegates representing the thirteen colonies had approved an agreement. They had declared that the colonies should not belong to England anymore. They said that the colonies should be free.

It was a popular decision with many people. But it was not at all popular with others.

"We shall at last be the authors of our own destiny," said one man behind Barbara, his voice pitched with emotion. "It is time. The King of England has abused us for way too long, John. We can't let them tax us without giving us a voice in our own government. We can't let them fight us and kill us like a greedy owner would punish his slave! We are not slaves, sir. We are men."

But the other man said, "I cannot listen to you, Stephen. We are Englishmen and we must handle our disagreements with manners and dignity, like Englishmen. I can't believe the delegates all agreed to tear us from our mother country."

"Manners have gotten us nowhere," said the man called Stephen. "The King has no respect for our manners."

"Look around you," said John. "See who it is who come out with such enthusiasm to hear the disloyal statement read. They are the ragged commoners! You won't see any of the finer folks among them. Rebels, all. I am going to take my family back to England. I cannot live in a place that so disregards her King."

"And I," said Stephen, his voice rising. "I cannot live while such torments are inflicted upon my countrymen! I shall personally take up arms and join our soldiers in the fields!"

With an exasperated growl, John pushed past Barbara and Patsy, trotting ahead, his tricornered hat bouncing.

Patsy leaned over to Barbara. "This shall be an exciting meeting, I tell you. Tempers are hotter today than I've seen them yet."

"I shall never forget today," Barbara replied. "Today, we are a new country."

"We are, indeed," Patsy said. "Some will be glad, others will be angry." Then she said, "I wonder about the girl you saw hiding under the trees at the silversmith shop yesterday. Would she care that we are now Americans?"

Barbara shrugged. "I don't know," she said. "The girl was so frightened."

"Maybe she'll come out to hear the reading of the declaration. Then you can point her out to me!"

"No," said Barbara. "She won't be there. She was too scared to be seen. I doubt I'll ever set eyes on her again."

The grounds of the State House were packed. It looked as though there were thousands of citizens, pushing and squeezing among each other. The noon sun was directly ahead, baking the heads of those who had come to hear the speech. Barbara and Patsy, like their mothers and most all other women, wore broad summer hats to keep sunlight off their faces. It was considered unattractive for a girl to have skin darkened by the sun.

Barbara's hat was a simple straw bonnet with a fresh handful of daisies tucked into the hatband. Patsy's was more elegant than Barbara's, with lace trim and a ribbon of blue velvet. It was tied neatly over Patsy's blond hair, shading her nose and her blue eyes.

The two families stopped at the back of the crowd, standing nearly at the road. Mr. Black and Mr. Layman stood beside each other, talking quietly. Mrs. Black and Mrs. Layman also stood together, playing with little Dorcas, who was awake and cooing.

"I can't see!" said Nicholas, tugging on the hem of his mother's dress. He was a slim, blond boy with blue eyes, much like his sister. He wore stockings, a hat, and breeches as did his father and older brother. "Can't we go up closer? I want to see, Mother."

Mrs. Black looked around and said, "Where is Henry? He could take you closer."

But Nicholas said, "He saw that girl he likes, Spencer Marie Thompson. They went off, laughing and talking."

Mrs. Layman's eyes widened. "So Henry has found a young lady he fancies?"

Mrs. Black said, "I do not know, Della. She is the daughter of the very wealthy Thompson family, who support the King most fervently. My Henry wants independence from the King. What he and Spencer talk about is beyond me. But she is a pretty girl, and witty and bright. They met at one of our tavern's dances in May."

"I see," said Mrs. Layman, nodding and smiling.

"Mother!" said Nicholas. "Hold me up so I can see!"

"I can't hold you, Nicholas. I've got Dorcas."

"Then let me go to the front!"

Mrs. Black said, "I'm sorry, Nicholas. You'll have to stand with us. Quit fidgeting so."

But Barbara interrupted, saying, "Mrs. Black, Patsy and I will be glad to take Nicholas closer. We will watch him carefully."

Patsy's mouth fell open. "We will?"

"Certainly, we will," said Barbara. She wanted an excuse to go to the front, too.

Mrs. Black said to Mrs. Layman, "Will that be all right with you, Della?"

"Of course," said Mrs. Layman. "But, Barbara . . ." She gave Barbara a look that Barbara had seen many, many times. It meant, *You behave yourself and don't get into any trouble.*

"Don't worry, Mother," Barbara said. "We'll be good!"

She took one of Nicholas's hands, and Patsy took the other. Nicholas squirmed, but Patsy said firmly, "You stay with us or we'll bring you right back!"

The three pushed their way through the wall of men and women and children. Nicholas whined but didn't try to get away. At last they came out into a small clearing, at the foot of a platform that had not been on the lawn before.

"You can let go of me now," said Nicholas. "I'm not a baby."

Barbara looked at Patsy. "Should we? You know your brother better than I do."

Patsy gave Nicholas a stern look. "If I let go of your hand, will you promise to stay right here? There are so many people here I'd never find you if you wandered off."

"I promise," said Nicholas.

"Is that a real promise or a pretend promise?" Barbara pressed.

Nicholas stomped his foot. "A real promise."

"All right, then," said Patsy. She let go of the hand she held. Barbara let go of the other one. Nicholas, luckily, remained where he stood.

And then Barbara heard a shout passing through the crowd. At first she couldn't understand what it was, but then she recognized the words. "Colonel John Nixon! He's coming with some members of Congress. Make room! Make room!"

The people parted, and several men came through. They were silent and solemn. One, dressed in a green waistcoat and brown hat, ascended the steps to the platform. There was a rolled paper beneath his arm. As soon as he situated himself, facing the street, the crowd went quiet. Only a few barking dogs and crying babies could be heard.

"I am Colonel John Nixon," said the man in a strong, steady voice. "And I am here to share with you a declaration that was approved four days prior by the Continental Congress. You have heard of this event, as it has already been printed in our newspaper. Yet we gather here to share and affirm its contents."

Barbara couldn't stop grinning. She and Patsy had been at the State House on July 4th when the Congress members had at last agreed on and signed Thomas Jefferson's declaration. And now they would hear what it said!

Patsy gave Barbara a wink, then looked back at the man on the platform.

Colonel Nixon adjusted the reading glasses on his nose, unrolled the scroll, and read, "In Congress, July 4, 1776. The unanimous declaration of the thirteen united states of America."

United States of America, Barbara thought. *I like the way that sounds!* It was clear Patsy liked it, too. She leaned over to Barbara and whispered in her ear, "Our country has a new name! And a fine name it is!"

Barbara nodded, then held up her finger to quiet

Patsy so she could hear what the Declaration had to say.

Colonel Nixon continued. "When in the course of human events, it becomes necessary for one people to dissolve the political bands which have connected them with another, and to assume among the powers of the earth, the separate and equal station to which the laws of Nature and of Nature's God entitle them, a decent respect to the opinions of mankind requires that they should declare the causes which impel them to the separation. . . ."

The Declaration continued, giving reasons the colonists should be free and independent, laying out the many tyrannies King George of England had wielded over those colonists. Not a minute after Colonel Nixon had concluded the reading, most of those listening erupted into loud cheers. Men of the militia tossed their hats and fired their weapons into the air in celebration. The bell in the State House began to ring. And then, over all the noise, Barbara could also hear church bells joining in from across the city. The flag atop the State House, the colorful King's Arms with its unicorn and lion, was lowered, carried by shouting men to a barren place on the lawn and set afire. Barbara and Patsy went over and watched as the flag curled up in the flames, then was reduced to ash.

"Good-bye," Barbara said quietly. She felt odd for a moment, watching the past burn, not certain what the future would hold, except for fighting and dying. Would the American soldiers and sailors truly be mighty enough to defeat the British? *I'm certain many are wondering the same thing,* she thought.

Some men walked away in disgust at the treasonous act of flag burning. But many stayed and watched until the ashes were caught in a breeze and blew away. These men laughed with joy.

Patsy leaned over to Barbara and whispered, "We must have a meeting of the Daughters of Liberty soon. We can help make bandages and gather herbs and medicines to send to the troops. The fighting will grow ever more fierce now that our Congress has declared us independent."

"You are right, Patsy," Barbara began. But then she glanced about and said, "Where is Nicholas?"

Patsy's mouth dropped open. "Oh, gracious! We've lost my brother! And I promised I would keep an eye on him."

"Yes, but he promised he would stay next to us," said Barbara. "He is as much at fault as we are."

"You go there," said Patsy, pointing at the east end of the lawn. "And I'll go the other way. If you find him, grab him and don't let go even if he screams."

"I won't," said Barbara. She wormed her way through the folks who remained, singing and cheering, on the State House lawn. How irritating to have to look after a seven-year-old boy when there was important patriotic work to do. In the late spring, Barbara and Patsy had formed a secret club they named the Daughters of Liberty. They had had several adventures so far. They had carried a spy's message to the Congress, and they had discovered an arsonist who had been burning businesses owned by patriots, and were crucial to his arrest. They had even given food to a very hungry and very tired Thomas Jefferson on the day that the Declaration was signed.

Now we have to chase after Patsy's little brother, Barbara thought ruefully.

The crowd began, at last, to disperse. As Barbara looked back and forth, studying clusters of people walking from the lawn to the street, she heard her mother call, "Barbara Layman! Come, daughter. We must return home. There is work to do!"

Barbara's Escape

"Nicholas! Nicholas Black!" Barbara shouted. "Where are you? You best come out of hiding now!"

She stopped, her arms crossed, scanning the area. Most folks were gone for the day, but she couldn't see Nicholas. She did see her own mother and father, along with the Black family, standing impatiently on the street.

Patsy caught up to Barbara. "Have you seen him?" she asked. "He can't be lost. He was with us only five minutes ago."

"How long does it take a boy to lose himself?" asked Barbara. "Maybe he doesn't want to be found, and then the two of us will be in trouble for his own prank."

"Nicholas!" they both called at the same time.

And then a voice from above said, "I am a member of Congress, and I have an important message to the citizens of Philadelphia!"

Barbara and Patsy looked up at the platform. Nicholas stood there, his chin tilted up in an air of haughtiness. He waved his hat in one hand. The free hand was pressed to his chest as if he were reciting a most important statement.

"Nicholas, come down here!" Patsy called.

"I am the honorable Nicholas Charles Black, at

your service," said Nicholas. "I declare today to be a day of freedom for all boys under ten years of age. They should be given their leave by their parents and allowed to swim in the river, play with their hoops, and eat all the pastries they can hold without any scolding. Today, my fellow men, is official Boys' Day. Let them do whatever they want, eat as much as they want, stay up as late as they want. This is my declaration!"

Barbara giggled, but Patsy was clearly angry.

"You'll be in trouble," Patsy said. "You and me both."

With a loud laugh, Nicholas hopped down the platform steps and raced across the lawn to his parents. Patsy and Barbara followed him at a slower pace.

Back at the tavern, Patsy bid Barbara good-bye before she went inside. "I have to help Mother and Katherine prepare the afternoon meal. Maybe after that, I'll have some time to meet and talk about our Daughters of Liberty plans!"

Barbara said, "Come to the stable when you are finished."

Patsy and her family went into the front of Black's Tavern. Mr. Black was the owner of the

Barbara's Escape

establishment, and his family worked hard to keep the place running smoothly for the guests who came to stay. It was a two-storied building, wide and long, with white clapboard siding and red shutters on the windows. Sometimes Barbara thought it must be fun to live there and to see and hear so many interesting guests talk over dinner in the Ulysses Room. But most of the time, Barbara knew she wouldn't be willing to trade her life for Patsy's. She was happy right where she was.

Barbara and her parents took a shortcut through the side garden to the back walk, which led past the tavern's detached kitchen, the hooded well, a small grove of apple trees, and the burned-out hull of what used to be Mr. Norris's blacksmith shop. Last week, it was burned down because Mr. Norris had refused to make tools for the British soldiers. What a frightening thing, seeing the smoke and flames engulf the building, threatening to leap over and destroy the stable as well.

But Barbara and Patsy had discovered who had done the terrible deed, and had reported it to the authorities. The man who had set the fires had been arrested.

"Go upstairs and put your bonnet away," said Mrs. Layman as they reached the stable. "Feed the horses and then join me in the vegetable garden. There's weeding to be done."

Barbara hurried up the wooden steps inside the stable to the two rooms her family shared. Just outside the door at the top of the steps, she wiped her shoes off on a rough mat, then opened the door and went inside.

The Layman home was simple, consisting of a front room in which the family ate, visited, read, and did lap work such as knitting, needlepoint, and mending. Barbara's mother had tried to teach Barbara these skills, but Barbara was not very good at them. Even Patsy had sat with Barbara in the side garden on many occasions, showing her once again how to make neat, tiny stitches in a torn apron or stocking.

"I'd rather work in the stable," Barbara had said many times, needle or hook in hand. "My fingers just want to go all over the place. They are determined that I am not to sew or knit. How can I argue with my hardheaded fingers?"

The second room was the family bedchamber. There was a bed for Mr. and Mrs. Layman and a small straw-stuffed mattress on the floor for Barbara. This room had a fireplace with several pewter candlesticks on the mantel. There was also a rock-

huddled against the wall, was the girl from Mr. Ford's backyard.

It was easier to see her now. She was a little younger than Barbara, and her cheeks were hollow, as if she'd not eaten well in a long time. She still wore no shoes, and she shivered as if she were cold, even on this hot day. But when she looked up at Barbara, her eyes, though ringed with tears, were determined.

"Hello, again," said Barbara. "Who are you?"

The girl took a deep breath. Her voice was clear and controlled. "My name's Gemmy. And yours is Barbara Layman."

"Yes," said Barbara. "I live here at this stable. Where do you live?"

"Nowhere."

"What do you mean? Everyone lives somewhere."

The girl slowly shook her head. "I don't."

Barbara remembered her mother, waiting in the vegetable garden for her. How long until she came looking? "Gemmy, why are you here in the stable? How did you find me?"

"Back the other day you told me your name and where you lived. I remembered. I'm not stupid."

"I didn't think that."

"A lot of people do," said Gemmy. "I can't read or write but I'm smart."

"I can't read or write, either," said Barbara. "At least, not very well."

"Why not?"

"I never tried very hard," Barbara answered.

"I never got the chance to learn."

A call came from beyond the stable. It was Mrs. Layman. "Barbara, come on now! These weeds are growing as I wait!"

Barbara looked back at Gemmy. "Why are you hiding?"

But Gemmy shook her head. "I can't say. You'll tell on me."

"You know I won't. I could have told Mr. Ford and I didn't. I could have already shouted for my father, but I haven't."

"No," said Gemmy. "You haven't . . . yet. But you don't know why I'm hiding."

Barbara held up her hand. "I promise, Gemmy. I swear I won't tell."

Gemmy stood up at last, slowly, stretching out her arms and legs. Her dress was very dirty and torn. There was a long scratch down Gemmy's dark face. "You shouldn't swear," she said. "My mama says swearing is bad."

From outside, Mrs. Layman called, "Barbara? Hurry!"

"Then I promise," said Barbara. "And I never break a promise."

Gemmy tightened the scarf's knot at the back of her neck. Then she said, "Have you ever seen a black girl before?"

"Well, certainly. There is a black boy at Dr. Willard's. He cleans the store. There is a black girl over at the saddlemaker's. She helps tan the leather, and then there is—"

"Have you ever met a black slave?"

"A slave? Gracious," Barbara said. "I've seen some passing through the city with their masters. But I've not spoken to one."

"You are speaking to one now," said Gemmy.

"You? You are a slave?"

"I was, four weeks ago. Then I came north."

"You ran away?"

"Yes. And if I'm caught and taken back, they'll beat me hard enough to rip the skin off my back. Look." Gemmy pointed to the scar on her face. "One time my mistress thought I was planning on running away. Two years ago this was, when I was nine. I was only going to the river to play, but she thought I was running. She struck me in the face with her husband's belt. The buckle cut my face so bad you could see the white of my jaw and teeth through the opening."

Barbara shuddered. How could anyone treat another person that way?

"And so I can't be caught. Never," said Gemmy. "I'd rather die than be a slave."

"Barbara!" It was Mrs. Layman. She was closer now, coming to the stable from the garden. Her voice was not happy.

"I must go!" said Barbara. "Hide here. I'm the only one who does the feeding, and Father won't need to refill the barrels because he did it only yesterday. Stay here and I'll bring you something to eat as soon as I can."

With that, Barbara dashed from the stable and across the paddock, just as her mother, with a frown on her face and her hands on her hips, reached the paddock gate.

4

Weeds grew quickly in a hot Philadelphia summer. Barbara and her mother, on their knees in the soil, tugged stubborn thistles, dandelions, and crabgrass from between the rows of beans and peas and cabbages. They tossed the weeds into buckets. These would be fed to Little Bit when they were through.

"Mother," said Barbara as she clawed her hands deeply, trying to free a hardy crabgrass root. "Have you ever met a slave?"

"Yes," said Mrs. Layman. "Of course. My parents owned several slaves back in Virginia."

Barbara dropped the crabgrass into the bucket and picked a tiny rock from under her fingernail. "What did you think of owning slaves?"

"I didn't think about it. It was something we did. Something many of our friends did."

"Didn't you think it was bad?"

Mrs. Layman paused, holding up a clump of clover with tiny white flowers. "Why are you asking all these questions? You've never been interested before."

Barbara shrugged. "I was just wondering."

Mrs. Layman made a soft tsking sound with her lips, then said, "I thought there was nothing wrong with it. But now, since I've grown up, I've come to realize that we were wrong. It is never right for one person to own another. It is against moral reason."

"I would hate to be a slave," said Barbara. "If I was one, I'd run away for certain."

"I'm sure you would, daughter," said Mrs. Layman.

"Hello, ladies." It was Mr. Layman. He was at the fence that surrounded the garden, leaning on the top railing. His hat had been pushed back on his head. "How grow the beans?"

"Fine," said Barbara. "But the weeds grow just as fine, and a good crop of them we have. Too bad we don't eat weeds. We could have a feast every day of the season."

Mr. Layman smiled, then looked out across the garden to the alley. His smile faded. His eyebrows drew together.

"Father," asked Barbara. "What's wrong?"

Her father hesitated, as if he didn't want to speak whatever was on his mind.

"Paul," said Mrs. Layman. "What is it?"

"You must leave Philadelphia," Mr. Layman said.

"On a holiday, Father?" asked Barbara. "Where are we going?"

"Not a holiday." Mr. Layman pulled his hat back straight on his head and closed his eyes briefly. Barbara could see his shoulders rise and fall.

"Then what?" asked Barbara's mother.

"I want you and your mother to move away from this city," he said at last. "I want you to stay with my sister, Susannah, in Lansdale."

Barbara was on her feet in a second. Weeds she had tucked into her apron fell to the ground. "Leave here? Move away? Why? We cannot, Father. I don't want to leave Black's Tavern! This is my home!"

"Paul," said Mrs. Layman, "why have you made such a hasty decision? This is the first you've mentioned it."

Mr. Layman pushed open the garden gate. It swung back in place, pulled by the weight of an iron ball hanging from a chain. He walked over to his family and sat right down in the dirt. He took both his wife's and his daughter's hands. "It's not a decision I make lightly," he said. "But I've been talking with some friends and, now that the Declaration of Independence has been signed, read, and cheered by our citizens, we feel that the British soldiers might come after Philadelphia with a vengeance. This is the city that houses Congress, the men who declared us free from the King. Do you not think the British will now find our city a prime target for their musket balls and cannon fire? Surely, the King hates Philadelphia more than any other city in any other colony."

"But the fighting is up in New England," said Mrs. Layman. "Near Boston."

"For now," said Mr. Layman. "But for how long? Who can say? I feel it could well become dangerous, and soon."

Barbara couldn't believe her ears. Leave her home? She'd lived in Philadelphia for three years and had thought it was where she would stay until she grew up. "We can't go," Barbara said. "We'll be careful, Father, we promise. I won't take Little

Bit out on the streets alone. I will always go with Mother or Patsy. We'll be very, very cautious."

"I'm sorry, Barbara," said Mr. Layman.

Mrs. Layman put her arm around Barbara, but Barbara tugged away. She crossed her arms over her knees and buried her face. It wasn't fair!

"Barb," said Mrs. Layman, "there is more to consider. Not only is it dangerous here, but you know I haven't been able to find new employment since I left Boxler's Milliner. It is hard for your father to keep us fed and clothed. Your father is right."

"No, he isn't. We're doing fine! If the British come here, they come. We can't escape it."

"You will have a better chance away from here," said Mr. Layman. His voice was firm. There would be no way to change his mind. "You and your mother must go where fighting is less likely. I am sending you to stay with your aunt Susannah. We will pack and leave tomorrow afternoon."

Barbara felt hot tears well in her eyes, but she blinked them back and asked, "Why do you keep saying Mother and I? What are you going to do?"

"I must stay here at the tavern. It's my responsibility. Mr. Black needs help with the horses."

Barbara spun around and in a trembling voice

said, "But Mother and I are your responsibility, too!"

"And that is why I'm making plans for your safety, daughter. That is most important to me."

Barbara looked at her mother. "Don't make us go—please!"

But Mrs. Layman only smiled a small, sad smile and said, "We will pack this evening. Don't make this harder than it already is, Barbara."

Mr. Layman went back to the stable, and the rest of the weeding was done in silence.

At last, the garden was cleared and Barbara had five full buckets to take to Little Bit. Mrs. Layman carried two and Barbara carried three, one in each hand and one over her elbow. She was so mad she couldn't speak to her mother. They went inside the stable and dumped the weeds in Little Bit's stall.

"Tasty treats," said Mrs. Layman as she reached out to scratch the pony's face. "We worked hard for these, you should appreciate them." She laughed, but Barbara didn't. She couldn't. She was too angry.

Mrs. Layman went upstairs to do some mending, and Barbara was at last free for a little while, until the afternoon meal at four o'clock.

"I have to tell Patsy," Barbara said aloud to

herself as she rubbed Little Bit's neck and shoulder. "I must tell her that we have to move."

It was then that Barbara remembered the girl in the feed room. Gemmy, the runaway slave! Maybe she and Gemmy could run away together and hide! Gemmy was good at hiding. Barbara wouldn't be found and wouldn't have to go to Aunt Susannah's.

At the feed room door, Barbara called quietly, "Gemmy?"

There was no answer.

"Gemmy?"

There was only silence. Gemmy wasn't in the feed room anymore. Barbara searched behind each barrel and crate. She looked in every stall and in the tack room. Gemmy had left.

"Oh, Gemmy," Barbara said as she stood in the doorway of the stable, looking out at the paddock, the grove of apple trees, and the path leading to the tavern. "I didn't even bring you food as I promised. I'm sorry you ran off again. I hope you'll be safe, wherever you are."

Barbara thought about running off on her own, but it seemed very scary. Even though Barbara was a brave Daughter of Liberty, she knew it would be lonely and frightening. Thinking about being alone, hiding, looking for food and a place to sleep made her stomach hurt.

But then her stomach hurt just as much when she thought about moving away from Black's Tavern, away from her home, away from her best friend. There had to be a way to make things right again!

"I'll tell Patsy," Barbara said to herself with a sharp nod of resolve. "Perhaps Patsy will run away with me!"

Up the walkway she hurried, through the apple trees, and past the hooded well. Sitting on the step of the detached kitchen were Henry Black and the girl he fancied, Spencer Thompson. Henry was holding Spencer's hand, but he dropped it as soon as he saw Barbara.

"Hello, Barbara," said Spencer. "It's nice to see you again."

"Nice to see you," Barbara said, but she kept on walking.

"Won't you come talk with us?" Spencer asked. "Henry and I were discussing whether women should be able to own property after they are married. He says no. I say yes. What do you say?"

"Of course women should have that right," said

Barbara. She reached the gate to the side garden and pushed it open.

"Come back and tell us why," Spencer called good-naturedly. "For pity's sake, I could use someone on my side!"

Barbara ignored the request, and she could hear Henry and Spencer pick up the conversation themselves. Over the rosebushes and into the open window of the Black family bedchamber Barbara peered. She could see Patsy sitting on the hard-backed chair, working on a sampler. "Patsy!" she called.

Patsy looked up. "Barbara, hello. Are you here to play? Mother says I may have a little free time."

Barbara took a long, deep breath. "I've got news. Bad news."

Patsy lay the needlework down on the top of the family's trunk by the window and put her hands on the sill. "What?"

"Father says we have to move. He says we can't live in Philadelphia anymore."

"Move away?" Patsy quickly climbed through the window, trying not to let her apron catch on the branches of a red rosebush. She dropped to the side garden and pulled her apron free of one thorny stem. "You are teasing me, Barbara. Your father wouldn't leave here. I know he likes it. I've heard him say so!"

Barbara sat down with a thump beneath an oak tree and rested her elbows on her knees. The tree's trunk was lumpy against her back, but she'd sat here so many times—visiting with Patsy, playing, trying to read and write and discussing plans for the Daughters of Liberty—the rough bark felt like the touch of an old friend. She linked her fingers together and stared at them. Patsy, in her usual careful manner, tucked her skirt beneath her before she sat on the grass. Patsy reached for her friend's hand and gave it a tight squeeze.

"It's true," Barbara said finally. "He thinks it's too dangerous to stay in Philadelphia. He thinks the British soldiers will attack any day now because of the Congress's declaration."

"But we aren't leaving, we're staying," said Patsy. "I don't think Father would allow us to remain here if he thought something bad would happen to us."

Barbara shrugged. "Fathers don't always think alike, do they?"

Patsy shook her head slowly.

"Run away with me."

"No!"

"Please?"

"Barbara, don't be a goose. We can't run away. How dreadfully we would scare our families. How terribly they would cry for us!"

"I suppose," said Barbara. Then she said, "Do you think your father would talk mine into letting us stay? Maybe he would have something to say that could ease my father's worries. My father has a great deal of respect for yours."

"I don't know," said Patsy.

"Will you try?"

"Certainly," said Patsy. "I'll ask him now. He's in the Red Horse Room with some of the guests, playing cards. I hope he says yes."

Quickly, Patsy hopped back through the window and disappeared. Barbara picked up several acorn caps and tossed them up and down in her hand. Then she threw them at the stone wall separating the tavern's side garden from the garden of the next-door neighbor, Mrs. Brubaker. A chipmunk darted across the garden, pausing to peer at Barbara for a second before vanishing beneath some dry leaves by the wall. A tiny brown spider dangled in front of Barbara's face, its dragline attached to one of the tree's lower branches. Barbara blew on it gently and watched it sway back and forth.

A spider can live where he wants to, she thought. *Nobody tells him he has to go away and live with his old, grouchy aunt.*

Patsy came back out the window and jumped to the ground. By her face, Barbara knew right away what she was going to say.

"No," said Patsy. "He said it isn't his place to interfere with your father's plans."

Barbara picked up a stick and hurled it at the wall. It smacked a stone and fell into the flowers. "We have to go live with my aunt Susannah. She lives northwest, on a farm near the town of Lansdale."

"Your aunt Susannah," Patsy said. "Is she the one who never smiles? The one who thinks young ladies should speak only when spoken to, and never ride a horse or play a game?"

Barbara nodded.

"That's terrible."

Barbara nodded again and said, "I suppose we won't see each other anymore. I guess you won't be my best friend any longer." Barbara stood up and turned to leave the garden. She felt a hand catch her arm. She turned back. Patsy's eyes were red, and she was fighting not to cry.

"Don't say that, Barb," Patsy said softly. "You'll

always be my best friend, no matter where you live." She took Barbara in a long, warm hug. Barbara could no longer keep the tears back; they flowed freely down her face. "You will write to me when you can?" Patsy asked.

Barbara whispered, "Oh, yes, of course. I will probably spell everything wrong, but I'll get Mother to help me."

"I'll come help you pack. How soon must you move?"

"Father says tomorrow afternoon."

"Oh, bother," said Patsy. She stepped back from Barbara and wiped her face on the belled sleeve of her dress. "I must find a gift for you, for going away."

"Don't give me anything," said Barbara as she left the garden for the path to the stable. "Just promise you won't forget me."

5

The following afternoon came much too quickly. The Laymans' wagon, which was usually kept in the stable aisle, was drawn out into the paddock. Barbara helped her father carry many things from the upstairs rooms down to the wagon, including a trunk filled with linens and quilts, two wooden crates with Mrs. Layman's and Barbara's clothing, and a smaller box, lined with straw, which held most of the family's dishes. Mr. Layman would keep a single plate, one mug, and one fork, knife, and spoon for his own meals. Five of the six wool blankets belonging to the family were laid out in the back for Barbara to sit on during the journey. There were several buckets and a bag of grain to feed the horses on the long trip.

Barbara's Escape

Mr. Layman hitched Dan to the wagon, pulling the straps securely and tightening the buckles. Dan looked odd and bony beneath the leather harness, but he didn't seem to mind. He stood patiently while the Laymans finished their loading, with his eyes closed and his tail flicking an occasional fly.

Barbara led Little Bit from her stall and out into the paddock. The pony hesitated at the gate, and Barbara had to urge her through. It was as if she knew she was leaving for good. "Take one last look, girl," Barbara whispered in her pony's ear. "We won't be back." Then she tied Little Bit to the back of the wagon. Little Bit began pawing the ground, making a hole. Barbara didn't scold her.

Mr. Layman put his arm around his daughter's shoulders.

"What you told Little Bit isn't necessarily true," he said. "The war won't last forever. Who knows what the future may hold? You and your mother may join me again, or I may find myself joining you. Cheer up, Barb."

Mrs. Layman, checking the placement of the boxes one last time, added, "You never can be certain, Barbara. There are good things to come; there always are."

Barbara thought, *Not at Aunt Susannah's. She's just a mean old lady!* But she didn't say it.

And then there was a call from the path: "Don't go yet!" It was the entire Black family—Patsy, Henry, Nicholas, Mrs. Black, and Dorcas—coming down from the tavern. Even Katherine Ralston, the young tavern cook, and the two Anderson sisters, in their simple Quaker garb and severe black bonnets, came bearing food baskets and sad smiles. Mr. Black followed them all, leading a prancing chestnut horse with black mane and tail.

"What is this?" said Mr. Layman, smiling and throwing up his hands. "What a send-off! We feel like royalty!"

"We wouldn't let you go off without telling you good-bye," said Mrs. Black. She and Mrs. Layman hugged each other tightly, wiped away a few tears, and then stepped back to dab at their eyes.

"Be safe and write us a letter when you find the time," Mrs. Black said.

Katherine passed two food baskets to Mrs. Layman. The prim Anderson sisters handed Barbara a bucket of candles and soap. "God go with you," the sisters said in unison.

Katherine said, "We will miss you."

"You've all been wonderful friends," Mrs. Layman replied. "I will certainly keep in touch, as often as time allows. I hope letters will not be delayed because of the war."

Mrs. Black nodded.

Patsy gave Barbara a hug and pressed a piece of cloth into her hand. "It isn't much," she said quietly into her friend's ear. "But I made it really quickly. I stayed up nearly all night. Mother let me work even after everyone had gone to bed. Put it in your room at your aunt Susannah's, and think of me when you look at it."

It was a sampler, a piece of hemmed cloth with embroidery making a design of a rose, a pony, a tree, and the smiling face of a girl. Beneath the picture were the words "Barbara and Patsy, friends forever. D.O.L."

Barbara touched the letters. "D.O.L.?" she asked.

Patsy nodded and whispered, "Daughters of Liberty!"

Barbara smiled. "Of course!"

Mr. Layman then said, "Paul, I don't know how far your nag will get you. I know you have a fondness for old Dan, and he's been with you many years. But I suggest you let him stay here and enjoy his last days as any old gentleman should be allowed. I am giving you this new horse to take his place. He's strong-willed and temperamental, but has been trained at harness as well as the saddle. I believe that with your understanding of the equine mind, you will have him pulling like a gentleman before you are out of the city limits."

"No," said Mr. Layman. "This is too generous a gift. I cannot accept."

Barbara stared at the horse. It was indeed a beautiful creature. *You have to keep him, Father,* she thought. *He is lovely!*

"I insist," said Mr. Black.

"Andrew, this animal cost you plenty," Mr. Layman protested. "Just bid us a safe trip and I shall be back in three weeks."

"If you cannot accept him on your own behalf," said Mr. Black, "then perhaps you will accept him on behalf of your wife and child. You want to be certain you bring them to your sister's home as quickly as possible. Copper is the horse to get you there and back. And on your return, think how much swifter you will be able to get from place to place, from saddlemaker to harness shop to blacksmith. I tell you, Paul, it is actually a favor to me if you take this horse. You will be able to manage the stable more efficiently."

Both of Barbara's parents laughed. Mrs. Layman

climbed up onto the wagon's bench seat and said, "You make a good case for taking the animal. I'm surprised you are a tavern owner and not a lawyer."

"He is yours, then?" asked Mr. Black.

"He is, indeed," said Mr. Layman. With that, Mr. Black helped Mr. Layman unharness Dan and put Copper in his place. The young horse snorted and stomped his feet impatiently. Henry led the old horse back into the stable.

Good-bye, old boy, Barbara thought.

After more hugs and good-byes, the Layman family was off at last through the city, Copper prancing like a gentleman at a gala ball, his ears flicking back and forth to Mr. Layman's steady commands.

"Slow, boy, whoa there. No need to trot. Easy now."

The city passed away more quickly than Barbara wished. She wanted to look at it all and hold it so it wouldn't slip away. Boys chased each other with sticks, pretending to be at war, men and women in yards and on roadsides burned bonfires, sang, shot rifles, and danced in lingering merriment at the declared independence of their homeland. Several churches continued to ring their bells.

They are happy, Barbara thought. *They aren't going anywhere. They aren't running away. I want to stay here!*

But she knew saying so wouldn't do any good.

Shops, homes and churches, and familiar streets soon were gone, and the green countryside stretched out before them. The road became a one-lane, dusty path, heading northwest, following through forests and fields, up and down gentle hills and along riverbeds. Watching the new landscape roll by slowly, Barbara leaned against a crate in the back of the wagon, the toes of her shoes tapping against each other. She waved at a little boy sitting on a fence around a small farm; she made mooing sounds to a herd of cattle grazing on a green, sloping hillside. She clapped her hands to startle a flock of sparrows perched on a sycamore tree limb and watched as they rose together into the air, like noisy children chased from a strawberry patch. She called "hello" to a man fishing in the river beside the road. A little golden dog chased the wagon a short way, then trailed off to follow a squirrel into the woods.

Where is the war? she wondered. *I don't see any danger. Father is being too careful. I wish he would realize that.*

Several hours later, Barbara's back had grown tired and her shoulders were sore from jostling about in the bumpy wagon. She climbed up to the front of the wagon bed and tapped her father on the arm. "May we stop for a moment?" she asked. "The wagon is so rattly, my head feels like it's shaking loose."

Mrs. Layman said, "I think that is a good idea, Paul. The afternoon has grown long. Let's stop so we can stretch and have a bite to eat."

The wagon rumbled to the side of the road near a pond, and everyone climbed out. Mrs. Layman spread a blanket on the soft grass by the pond and opened the two baskets Mrs. Black had given her. Inside was a dinner, enough for a family twice the size of the Laymans'. Wrapped in linen napkins were apples, three wedges of cheese, biscuits, ham, dried beef, figs, raisins, two mince pies. As Mr. Layman tethered the horses and filled buckets of water from the pond for them, Barbara helped her mother set the food out on the blanket. They would eat on the linen napkins so they wouldn't have to unpack the dishes.

As the horses drank their water, the family settled with their own meal. Although Mr. and Mrs. Layman seemed to enjoy the food, talking happily between bites of ham and bread, Barbara couldn't enjoy it. The food had little taste and didn't sit well in her stomach.

I wonder what Patsy's doing, she thought as she chewed on a strip of dried beef. *I wonder if she's making the bandages for our soldiers without me. I wonder if she has found a secret message to take to the Congress or has discovered a ring of spies on Mulberry Street. Maybe she has told Abby Boxler about the Daughters of Liberty. Maybe Abby has taken my place. Oh, how I dread going to Aunt Susannah's!*

"Are you not hungry, Barb?" Mr. Layman pointed to her napkin, which was still full of food. "Mrs. Black went to a lot of bother for us. We should not waste it."

"I don't want to waste anything," Barbara answered. "But I can't eat."

I wonder what Gemmy is doing, Barbara thought. *Is she still hiding on the grounds of Black's Tavern? What will happen to her? What if she is caught and sent back?*

"Are you sick?" her mother asked.

Barbara shrugged. "I don't think so. I just don't feel well."

Mrs. Layman pulled her daughter into a warm

embrace. "I know what it is," she said. "And I know how you feel. You'll see Patsy again, I'm certain. Don't fret. Now please, have something to eat. It will make you feel better."

Barbara swallowed the beef she held in her teeth, but she didn't feel better at all.

Suddenly, she heard voices up the road, around a bend where a grove of cedar trees stood. Barbara and her parents paused, turning toward the sound. They were low men's voices. Even Little Bit, tied to the back of the wagon, stopped her snuffling of the ground when she heard them. She lifted her head and perked up her ears.

British soldiers! Barbara thought. *They are close by after all! They're going to take us as prisoners!*

But it was only two shabby men, dressed in dirty stockings, plain breeches, and jackets of coarse leather. Over their shoulders were slung satchels of leather. One wore a squashed tricornered hat. The other man's head was bare. Their hair was pulled back loosely with strings, and their noses were red with sunburn.

Mr. Layman stood and raised his hand in greeting. "Hello there, gentlemen! And from where are you traveling and how long?"

The man without the hat said, "We've been traveling several days. Since the weekend."

"Would you care to share a meal with us?" asked Mr. Layman. "We've more than enough."

The man with the hat said, "Thank you, sir. Our feet are tired and our bellies are growling. But we won't trouble to sit with you and your family. We'll take the food and move on."

"Nonsense," said Mrs. Layman. "Join us. We would enjoy the company."

The man with the hat rubbed his chin and said, "Why, thank you. That is mighty generous."

The men dropped their satchels to the ground and sat by the blanket, accepting with nods and smiles the napkins full of food that Mrs. Layman passed to them. The men, who said they were farmers, talked with Mr. Layman about weather and crops while Mrs. Layman listened politely. Barbara, bored with the conversation, walked around the pond, grabbing at the yellow butterflies and lacy-winged dragonflies, and flaking the tops of the cattails to let the downy seeds float into the air.

A huge bullfrog hopped to the edge of the pond and stared at Barbara. She stared back. He croaked. She put her hands on her knees and croaked back. He stretched his back legs and prepared to jump back into the water. As quickly as she could, Barbara scooped with her hands and caught the bullfrog around the stomach. "Ha!" she shouted. "I got you!"

And then her foot slipped on the muddy bank. She whirled her free hand, trying to keep from falling, but it didn't help. Like a clumsy ice skater, Barbara slid with a squawk into the knee-deep water of the pond.

"Oh!" she shouted. The water was cold; the mud was slimy. Her skirt and petticoat were wrapped tightly around her legs like cold wet leeches. Yet she didn't let go of the bullfrog.

"Barbara?" It was her mother, coming around the pond, peering through the cattails and milkweed. "Where are you?"

"In the pond."

"Gracious!" Mrs. Layman peeked through the grasses and shook her head. "Are you all right?"

"Yes," said Barbara. "But I can't get out."

"Then you are not all right."

"I will be," said Barbara. "As soon as I get out."

Mrs. Layman shook her head and sighed loudly. She walked to the edge of the pond, trying to keep her shoes from being caked with mud, and reached out. "Here, take hold. I'll pull you out."

Barbara took her mother's hand. In Barbara's free hand, the bullfrog struggled mightily. Mrs. Layman tugged, but Barbara's feet sank even deeper in the mire. Soon, the mud was up to her ankles.

"Let go of that frog," said Mrs. Layman, pushing up her sleeves. "I need both your hands to get you out."

"But he's such a fine frog," said Barbara. "He'll make a good pet to take to Aunt Susannah's. He can keep me company in my room."

Mrs. Layman laughed suddenly and shook her head. "I don't think Susannah will allow such a thing."

"But I will let him swim in the horse trough during the day and sleep in the washbowl at night. I won't let him get away, I promise. See how big he is? And I caught him!"

But Mrs. Layman's smile faded. "Barbara, you must get out of that water before you catch your death of chill. Aunt Susannah would no more let you keep a frog than she will let you ride . . ." Barbara's mother stopped, her lips pressing together.

"Ride what?"

"Ride astraddle like we let you back in Philadelphia. There are going to have to be some changes on our part, daughter, to please your aunt. After all, it is her home."

Barbara's mouth fell open. Her fingers loosened, and the bullfrog dropped into the pond with a plop. "You're teasing me."

"Give me your hands. You must get out of that water."

Barbara reached for her mother. With several tugs, Barbara got her feet free of the mud and up on the pond bank. Her mother took her shawl off and covered Barbara's shoulders, but Barbara couldn't feel it. All she could think was, *Aunt Susannah is going to tell me how I can ride Little Bit?*

"You've dry clothing in the wagon," said Mrs. Layman as she walked with Barbara back to the picnic blanket. "I will find a private spot behind some trees and help you change."

Aunt Susannah is going to have more say than my mother over what I do and don't do? No! I won't tolerate it!

Mr. Layman and the two men were standing, their faces set in a serious discussion. But they stopped talking when they saw Barbara.

"What happened?" asked Mr. Layman.

"She just went for a little wade," said Mrs. Layman. "You know our Barbara. We were just going to find her some dry clothes in the trunk. We won't be long. I know we need to get back on our way soon so we can reach your sister's before it grows dark."

But Mr. Layman held up his hand. "I'm afraid our plans have been changed."

"What do you mean?" asked Mrs. Layman.

"We won't be going to Susannah's after all," he announced.

"Hurray!" shouted Barbara, bouncing up and down until her mother put a restraining hand on her shoulder.

"Why not, Paul?" Mrs. Layman asked. "After all this work and thought, we're turning around?"

Mr. Layman sighed. "It seems we have no choice. Our new friends here used to live near Susannah's farm. They say the land is swarming with British soldiers, and they are destroying everything they come upon. Their own farms were razed to the ground. They escaped before they themselves were captured."

"Indeed? I thought the fighting was much farther north."

"Oh, but some is much closer, ma'am," said the man with the hat.

"How dreadful," said Mrs. Layman. "And what of your families, sirs? Are they harmed?"

The man with the hat said, "We have no families, only ourselves."

"And where are you going?" asked Mrs. Layman.

"To Philadelphia. It would be much safer for us, for everyone, to be in the city."

Mrs. Layman put her hand to her lips and said nothing for a moment. Then to her husband she said, "And us?"

"We shall return also," said Mr. Layman. "I could never take my family intentionally into such peril."

"That's wonderful!" Barbara said, forgetting her wet clothes. "Did you hear that, Little Bit? We're going back home!" She gave her pony a great big hug. Barbara was almost bursting with the excitement of seeing Patsy again.

6

The two men were invited to sit in the back of the wagon, and Barbara got permission to ride Little Bit alongside. She didn't put on the sidesaddle, but instead rode bareback, almost wishing her aunt were there to see her.

What would you say to me, Aunt Susannah? Would you tell me I could not ride my pony in such a way? I'm glad you aren't my mother!

The sky had clouded over, and the air smelled like a summer rain was on the way. But nothing could dampen Barbara's spirits. She was going back to Philadelphia. Back home, back to Patsy and her own room over the stable.

"You seem to be good with horses," said the

bareheaded man after the family had gone nearly a mile. "Your father tells me he works at a stable and you have many horses there to take care of. Fine, expensive animals belonging to the tavern guests."

"Yes," said Barbara. "I know all about horses."

"Nice pony you have there," said the man with the hat. "She seems very strong, as strong as a mule."

Barbara pulled up close to the wagon's side. "Oh, yes," she answered. "She's very strong. Stronger than a horse. Little Bit could pull this whole wagon by herself if we didn't have Copper. But she's no mule—she's a real lady."

The man without the hat said, "I see. A strong lady—unusual combination."

"And," Barbara said, letting go of the reins with one hand and rubbing her pony on the shoulder, "she is very smart. Smarter than some people I know, even people who have gone to college. I've taught her tricks. Watch this."

Barbara reached back and patted Little Bit twice on her rump. Without hesitation, the pony took four dainty skipping steps before moving back into a trot. Then, Barbara snapped her fingers. Little Bit nickered loudly.

"Such talent," said the man without the hat. "She must be worth quite a lot of money."

"Yes," said the other man. "How much would you say she was worth?"

"Oh, I don't know," said Barbara. "I would never think of selling her. She is my second-best friend. I'm going to keep her for the rest of her life."

The man with the hat said, "Oh, I can see you are friends. Take good care of that pony. You would hate to have her lost or stolen."

"That would be dreadful," Barbara said.

"It would be, indeed," said the man without the hat.

"There are other tricks Little Bit can do when I'm not on her back," said Barbara. "Maybe when we get to the city I can show you."

Both men nodded. Barbara smiled. But then she noticed something strange. The man without the hat had lowered his hand beside him and made strange motions with his fingers. The other man cast his eyes downward and watched the other's fingers intently.

What is he doing? Barbara wondered. She didn't want to act as if something was odd, because clearly the men were doing something in secret, something they didn't think she would notice. But the motions looked like some sort of code. Barbara glanced away when the man's hand became still. She didn't want him knowing she was suspicious.

"How are you faring back there?" Mr. Layman called to the passengers.

"Fine, sir, and thank you very much," said the man without the hat. "Our feet would thank you, too, if they could talk." Then he gave the other man a cold smile, crossed his arms over his knees, and stared at the road behind the wagon.

Barbara urged Little Bit into a trot, and they moved ahead of the wagon. She said nothing to her parents. Maybe she had just imagined the finger code. Maybe he just had a cramp in his hands and had to wiggle them to work it out.

Maybe, she thought. *But maybe not.*

The clouds overhead grew heavier and darker. A few minutes later it began to sprinkle. Mr. Layman urged Barbara to tie Little Bit to the wagon and join the men in the back. "We've got blankets, daughter," he said. "It will keep the worst of the water off you."

But Barbara said, "I've been wet once today. I don't mind it again. May I please ride Little Bit the rest of the way?"

Mr. Layman agreed. *Good,* Barbara thought. *I don't want to sit with those men. I don't trust them.*

The rain drizzled steadily on as the family traveled the final miles to Philadelphia. Barbara felt a rush of relief and joy when they crested a knoll and saw the homes lying at the outskirts of the city. Copper and Little Bit both seemed to know that soon they would be in a dry, comfortable stable. It took all of Barbara's effort to keep her pony from breaking into a canter, and Mr. Layman's constant, "Hold there, boy," told Barbara he was having the same problem with Copper.

Streetlights were burning by the time the wagon reached Mulberry Street. Candles and lanterns blazed in shop windows, their glows made fuzzier by the water on the window glass. A few men walked along the street, hunched over in the rain, trying to keep from stepping in the puddles.

"May I go ahead?" Barbara asked her parents. From beneath a blanket Mrs. Layman was holding over herself and her husband, her mother said, "Yes. Go on. We'll catch up with you in a minute. Get a fire going in the fireplace."

"I will!" Barbara at last let Little Bit have what she wanted—her head. Loosening up on the reins and giving the pony's sides a tap with her heels,

Barbara leaned forward and held onto a handful of wet mane. Little Bit galloped the last block and turned into the alley that traveled behind Black's Tavern.

She hopped from the pony and urged her through the paddock gate. Then, as the raindrops grew larger and faster, she ran up the path toward the tavern.

The Blacks are probably in bed, she thought as she reached the backyard. *Would they be angry if I woke them up to say we're back?* She stood for a moment, looking at the windows of the tavern. Most were dark; she could see only two candles burning in upstairs bedchambers. And the window of the Black family's bedchamber had no light at all. Barbara opened the side garden gate and stood by the rosebushes. Through the window, she could hear Mr. Black snoring and baby Dorcas making little sleeping, cooing sounds.

I'll call softly, Barbara thought, shivering at last in the steady rain. *I have to let Patsy know I've returned.*

"Patsy?" she whispered.

There was no sound other than the baby, the snoring, and the pattering of the rain on the leaves in the side garden. "Patsy?" Barbara called a little louder.

Still, there seemed to be no movement within the family's room. Barbara stomped her foot on the wet grass. She always heard noises in the stable at night, and was always the one to wake up when a horse neighed or a man came singing down the alley at two in the morning. Her parents never heard such sounds. Was Patsy really as sound a sleeper as Mr. and Mrs. Black?

"Patsy Black, wake up!" Barbara shouted. And then she realized how loud she'd been. She put her hand over her mouth. "Oh, dear," she whispered.

Lanterns and candles were lit quickly in all the upstairs dormers of the tavern. She could hear men grumbling and calling out.

"What is that?"

"Who is that?"

"What is the commotion? Quiet, there. You'll wake the dead!"

Then a lantern glowed in the Blacks' bedchamber and was carried to the window. Barbara could see all the faces—Henry, Nicholas, Mr. and Mrs. Black, and Patsy—silhouetted in the flame, staring out at the drenched girl in the side garden in the middle of the night.

Patsy leaned farther through the open window than the rest of the family, and in a matter of seconds, her startled frown erupted in a wide grin.

"Barbara! You're here!"

"Yes!"

"Did you run off?" asked Mrs. Black. "Patsy said you didn't want to go. You didn't leave your parents, did you?"

"Oh, no, we're all home again," said Barbara. "Home to stay!"

"Wonderful!" said Patsy. "Oh, that is just marvelous! Father, Barbara is back to stay!"

Mr. Black chuckled. "Yes, we can see that."

"I'm so happy," said Mrs. Black.

"Me, too!" said Patsy.

Upstairs, from a window, a man shouted down, "We're all happy she's home! Now would you please give weary men some quiet so we can get some sleep?"

The Black family and Barbara were silent for a moment, then they all broke into laughter.

"Go to bed now, child," said Mrs. Black, her voice now quiet and soft. "Change your wet clothing and get a good night's sleep. I will give Patsy a little time in the morning to come visit you before her chores. Tell your mother I will come, too, to see her and bring you a morning meal."

"Yes, ma'am," Patsy said, curtsying in her soaking skirts. "Good night." As she opened the gate and walked down the path to the stable, she could hear men calling from the upstairs tavern windows.

"Good night!"

"Good night!"

"Good night, little girl! Welcome back!"

Barbara couldn't help but laugh again.

7

The stable was warm with the bodies of horses, the dry scents of straw and hay, and the soft voices of Barbara's parents. Mr. Layman took a blanket from the wagon, but said they would leave everything else loaded until morning, when they'd gotten a good night's sleep and had more energy to handle the boxes and crates. Barbara took Little Bit into her stall and rubbed her down with an old cloth. Then she followed her parents up the steps to the family's rooms. But voices made her stop and turn around.

"Hey, that's my spot."

"Don't be greedy. I claimed that place first. You can sleep by the window."

In the stall near the tack room, which tonight held no visitor's horse, were the two men who had traveled with the Laymans from the country. They grumbled at each other, kicking around straw, making piles on which to sleep.

"Are they staying here?" Barbara asked.

"Why, yes," answered Mrs. Layman. "We couldn't turn them out in the night rain, not after the warning they gave us."

"Why aren't they sleeping in the tavern?"

"We made that offer," said Mrs. Layman. "But they said they have never stayed in a tavern and would not be comfortable."

"But listen to them complaining down there. They don't seem to prefer the stable either."

Mrs. Layman laughed lightly. "Every person has his or her own peculiarities, daughter."

Barbara hesitated, then said, "I don't really trust those men. We really know very little about them."

"Barbara Layman," Mrs. Layman chastised, "we might well owe them our lives. The least we can do is offer them a warm stall for the evening."

Barbara's jaw tightened but she said nothing more.

Upstairs, the two rooms seemed to welcome Barbara like old friends. The smells of the fireplace and the candles were wonderful and warm. Mrs. Layman tucked the blanket around Barbara and sang a gentle song she had made up when Barbara was just a tiny girl.

> The day is like a rich man adorned in
>   golden clothes,
> But evening is a mistress fair with diamonds
>   on her toes.
> The night, she sings a whispering song with
>   breezes cool and kind.
> And all our cares will drift away when Lady
>   Night draws nigh.

Barbara felt her eyelids grow heavy in spite of the nagging sense that the men were downstairs, in her stable, in her home.

> The fields and streams are resting now, the
>   ox and horses, too.
> The farmer and his children stop their work
>   until the dew.
> And you, my daughter, sleep thee well for
>   well thou are so loved.
> May angels keep us all in sleep, with bless-
>   ings from above.

Barbara fell asleep to her mother's sweet melody. A dream came upon her, filled with horses and flowers and bright, warm sunlight. She was riding Copper, and then Sun Star, over a river and across a field. Other horses, free and without saddles or bridles, raced alongside her. She felt free, she felt happy.

And then, with a start, she awoke.

Barbara sat straight up on her mattress and tilted her head. She held her breath, trying to hear more clearly. There was movement down in the stable. Barbara was used to the stomping and nickering of horses, but this was something different. She thought she could hear men's voices.

Quickly, she stood and wiped her eyes. She would take a look quietly, without waking her parents. If it was only her imagination, set afire from the long previous day, then it was best to let them sleep. Slipping into her shoes and wrapping her shoulders with the shawl she'd left on the front room chair, Barbara opened the door and sneaked down the steps, carefully avoiding the one near the bottom, which creaked.

She could see flickering lantern light moving around near the tack room. The men were awake.

She could see their shadowy shapes moving, and that they were holding bridles and saddles.

What are they doing? That tack belongs to the guests at Black's Tavern!

Then Barbara saw that all of the family's possessions had been taken out of the wagon and placed by the stable wall. Copper had been hitched to the wagon in the stable aisle.

What is going on? she wondered. Her heart began to pound. Were these men planning on leaving, and taking the Laymans' horse and wagon? Were they common thieves?

I must tell Father!

But then she saw the men turn around. The lantern was being carried down the aisle toward her.

If I try to run up the steps, they will surely see me, she thought. Barbara quickly crawled beneath a blanket in the back of the wagon. She would hold still and make no sound or motion. As soon as the men moved away, she would get out and hurry upstairs.

The wool scratched her face. She could hear her breath; she could hear her heartbeats pounding in her ears. Were they loud enough for the men to hear, too?

Footsteps came close and stopped beside the

wagon. The voice that spoke was in a whisper, but clear enough to understand.

"We have to hurry. You finish loading the tack, and I'll string the horses together. I'll tie them to each other's halters with lengths of rope like a string of fish from the Delaware River! What a catch, eh? With luck, we can be out of here in five minutes!"

The second voice said, "And the Layman family will sleep through it. Careless fools! They deserve to have their horses stolen right from under their noses."

"Our captain will be pleased with us," said the first man. "Horses for the King! Maybe we'll be promoted."

"Maybe. Now, hurry. And keep silent."

They are stealing our horses! What shall I do? Barbara's body began to tremble. If she got up, what would they do to her? She had no choice but to remain beneath the blanket and to stay quiet. Never had Barbara been as frightened as she was at this moment.

And then, she heard a soft rumbling near her in the wagon. Someone was with her, hiding beneath another blanket. Who could it be? Was it another spy for the King? Was he going to catch her now, and take her out and hang her from the stable rafters?

Something was dropped on top of the blanket under which Barbara hid. *Saddles,* she thought. *And bridles. I have to get out of here, but how?*

"Come on now," said one man. "Hurry up. I'm ready to go. Tie those nags to the wagon and we must be off. We have but one night to get where we need to be."

Barbara again felt the movement near her, and then she heard a soft cough.

Gemmy? Is Gemmy hiding here in the wagon?

There was more thumping beyond the blanket, and several horses snorted. The front of the wagon shook as the two men climbed onto the seat.

"I'll drive," said one man.

"No, I'll drive," said the other. "I have more experience. I know more about horses. You just sit there and don't say anything. I don't want to have to listen to you hours on end. We have far to go, and I'm sick of your yammering already. I'll be glad when we are back with our regiment and I don't have to spend another minute with you." Then he made a clucking sound and ordered, "Get up there, mule."

With a jolt, Copper lunged forward and the

wagon went with it. Barbara rolled slightly and dug her fingers into the wood beneath her to keep still.

I'm being stolen, she thought. *Just like the horses! I have to get out of here!*

And then a hand grabbed her leg and it was all she could do to keep from screaming.

A whisper came from beneath the blanket next to her. "Barbara, is that you?"

"Yes," Barbara whispered. She lifted the blanket slightly and squinted into the darkness. She could see a face peeking back at her.

"What is happening?" asked Gemmy, her voice barely loud enough to hear. "Where are we going?"

"I don't know," Barbara answered. "Soldiers of the King are taking the horses from the stable. And we are trapped in the wagon with them!"

"Trapped," Gemmy repeated. "Oh, Lord, we are truly in danger."

"Yes. But if we are quiet and hold still, perhaps we can escape when they are not paying attention."

Gemmy crawled closer, moving beneath Barbara's blanket. "Move slowly," Barbara warned. "They mustn't see us!"

Once Gemmy had moved, the two girls could speak more easily. A strand of wool went up Bar-

bara's nose, and she pinched it to keep from
sneezing.

"I knew you and your family had left the stable," Gemmy said. "And so I thought I'd have
some days by myself, days when I could sleep in
your two rooms upstairs and pretend they were
mine. But then I heard you galloping into the yard
and I looked out. You were all back. As quickly
as I could I went back downstairs and hid in the
tack room again. I heard the men, but thought they
were just drifters."

"They aren't," Barbara whispered. "They are
horse thieves. As soon as my father told them that
we lived at a stable with valuable horses, they
knew what they would do. They were sent to scout
for horses for the British and we brought them
right here! I'm sure they lied about the fighting
near my aunt Susannah's. They only wanted to
come back with us, and we let them. My parents
trusted them!"

"Dreadful!" said Gemmy. "I waited until I
thought everyone had gone to sleep, then came out
of the tack room to find a blanket. There was one
in the back of the wagon. But then I heard you on
the steps, and so I covered myself up and waited,
hoping you'd go back to bed."

"And I saw the men coming closer and I had to hide, too."

"So here we are," Gemmy said, "trapped."

Barbara swallowed. It hurt her throat. "Yes, here we are." But she refused to say "trapped."

The wagon hit a bump, and Barbara heard one of the men say, "Watch where you are going, you fool. We've got six horses and one pony tied up to this wagon. We can't afford to have any of them twist a leg in a hole and break a leg."

Pony? Barbara thought. *Not only have they stolen the guests' horses, they've stolen Little Bit, too!*

"Do you want a turn at the reins?" asked the other man. "I'd be just as happy to sit and do nothing but complain while you drive this berserk horse through the streets. You can see he is a handful, and I imagine you would rather me do the work while you enjoy the view."

The other man didn't answer.

The girls said nothing to each other for what seemed like a very long time. Gemmy coughed occasionally, and Barbara found herself picking at the blanket to try to keep her mind off the terrible danger into which she had put herself. What if her parents woke up and found her missing? What if the men decided to looked beneath the blankets and found two girls hiding there?

We have to get out of here!

Surely the men would stop soon. Surely they wouldn't drive on forever. Surely they couldn't!

But Copper was in the harness, and the men were clearly under orders to steal horses and deliver them in haste. It could be a very long time before they stopped to rest.

And they would be many, many miles from Philadelphia by then.

8

Barbara's eyes wanted to close and let her sleep, but her thoughts wouldn't let them.

If we slow down, I'll climb out of the wagon. Then I can jump behind a tree or barn and hold still until the thieves are way out of sight.

But then she thought, *And what of Gemmy? I can't leave her. And I don't think two of us can sneak out without the men seeing us. And what of Little Bit? Can I leave her with these terrible men?*

On and on the wagon rumbled through the night. The heat beneath the blanket was barely tolerable. Barbara's neck and arms were covered with sweat. She reached out and found Gemmy's hand. "Don't worry," she said. "We'll get away somehow. I'm a Daughter of Liberty. We are brave and clever in times of trouble."

"What is a Daughter of Liberty?" asked Gemmy.

"It's a secret," said Barbara. "But when we escape, I'll tell you, all right?"

"All right."

The wagon went down an incline, and Barbara could hear splashing. The wagon shook as it rocked over stones. *We're crossing a shallow river,* Barbara thought. *I must remember this when we get away, so we can try to find our way back home.*

And suddenly, one of the men said, "Horses are getting tired, Gabriel. We must take a rest and let them have water. I need to rest a few moments, too. This wagon is dreadful. I think the wheel is coming loose."

But the other man said, "The wheel is not loose. And we cannot stop, Anthony. We must complete this trip under cover of night."

Anthony sounded irritated. "Shall we, then, deliver lame horses to our captain? I would not want to see the anger on his face!"

"They are not lame. These are healthy animals."

"But for how long? Any man knows a horse must be well cared for if he is to serve his master."

"I cannot worry about that," said Gabriel. "We must be at camp in all good haste."

"The animals cannot go at such a pace! They will be in dire stress when we make it to camp."

"They will not!"

"Yes, they will. Your mind is mush, Gabriel! And what will broken horses say of us, of our ability to do an important task? It will say that we know nothing of horses and should be nothing more than drummers or fife boys!"

As the men argued, Barbara noticed that the wagon was slowing down. Gabriel and Anthony were so intense with their words, it was obvious they hadn't noticed that Copper had decided a walk was more comfortable than a trot.

"Why did I get paired with you, you moron," said Anthony. "You are more of a complainer than a woman!"

"You are more of a complainer than a girl!"

Barbara gritted her teeth. Not only were these men thieves and British soldiers, they also knew nothing about girls.

They will be surprised when two girls outwit them and steal the horses back without their knowledge!

Copper's pace grew even slower, Barbara noticed. *If we can get out now we can hide, then sneak*

Barbara's Escape

behind the wagon and untie the horses. Barbara tapped Gemmy on the shoulder. "Get ready," she said to the girl. "We are going to roll out from under the blankets and out of the wagon."

Gemmy's eyes widened as if she wasn't certain, but she nodded anyway. Barbara pushed with her toes, moving beneath the irregular and lumpy weight of the saddles and bridles, until her fingers found the unlatched back of the wagon. Gemmy inched up behind her.

Barbara poked her head from beneath the blanket. The night was dark; the only light was from the lantern Gabriel and Anthony had in the front. Clomping behind the wagon, some with heads hanging down and others with ears twisted back in frustration, were six horses and Little Bit. Little Bit appeared to be limping on her right front leg. Already, she was weary and sore.

"Now," said Barbara. She rolled from the back of the wagon, landing on her feet and jumping clear of the horses. She bent over so the men wouldn't see her and followed the wagon as it continued ahead.

Come on, Gemmy. Roll out now! she urged.

But as Gemmy's face came out from under the blanket, Gabriel said, "Look how we've slowed down, Anthony. Give me those reins and let me drive this lazy animal. We must pick up speed, regardless of your grievances."

"Gabriel . . ." Anthony began. But there was the slap of reins against Copper's back, and with a shudder and jerk, the wagon lunged forward. Copper was trotting again.

Oh, no! Still hunched over, Barbara ran after the wagon. The horses tied to the back pounded along, keeping up. Little Bit whinnied in complaint but had no choice but to trot along.

Barbara grabbed for the wagon's side, but it pulled free of her grasp as Copper picked up an even faster pace.

No. Slow down! I can't be left alone. I can't lose Gemmy. I can't lose the horses! she pleaded silently.

Grabbing the wagon again, she held it for a moment, but a bump tossed her free. She stumbled, slamming into one of the horses in the front of the line. She was knocked away and thrown into the thorny weeds at the side of the road.

Surely the men have seen me! she thought. *Oh, please, I hope they have not seen me!* She was on her feet again and could see that the wagon had put many yards between it and herself in just those few seconds. Panting, Barbara leaned over and ran after it, keeping away from the stamping horses' hooves. She reached the wagon, grabbed the side, and swung herself up and over. As she landed in the back, she wormed her way beneath the blanket and lay there, gasping.

Gemmy crawled beside Barbara. "Why are you back? You were away. You were free."

"I had to come back," Barbara managed.

"But why?"

"Because I'm a Daughter of Liberty. And that means freedom for all, not just one."

Gemmy took a deep breath. She said nothing for a moment, then replied, "Thank you. Thank you, Barbara."

Barbara said, "You're welcome."

They stayed silent for many, many minutes. Barbara's arms and legs were tight with worry. Little Bit was going lame. They were going farther and farther from Philadelphia. They were only feet away from two British soldiers who were stealing horses for their fellow soldiers.

"Are you hungry?" Gemmy asked. Her face was close to Barbara's, and she was holding the blanket up a bit so it would be easier to breathe.

"Certainly," said Barbara. "But there is no use

thinking about it. Who knows when we shall be able to eat again?"

"I've food with me," said Gemmy. She bumped around, then held something out to Barbara. "Bread and ham," she said. "I had it in my skirt pocket."

"Where did you . . . ?" But Barbara realized that Gemmy had found some of the leftover food the Laymans had left in the wagon overnight. Maybe Gabriel and Anthony had tossed the family's belongings out to make room for the saddles, but Gemmy had discovered the baskets and had helped herself to leftovers.

That is exactly what I would do. Gemmy is resourceful. I suppose she's had to be. Together we will escape. Together we will get away from these bad men and go home.

But as Barbara took a bite of the ham, she thought, *I will go home. But Gemmy has no home.*

Barbara remembered the words of the Declaration of Independence, read by Colonel Nixon to the crowd on Chestnut Street: "To assume among the powers of the earth, the separate and equal station to which the laws of Nature and of Nature's God entitle them . . ."

Gemmy did not deserve to be a slave. She deserved to be free from her owners. She deserved the equal station to which the laws of nature and of nature's God entitled her.

I wonder if Gemmy could live with us? Barbara thought. *I wonder if Father and Mother would let her stay and be part of our family? I always wanted a sister. I will tell them so when we get home again.*

If *we get home again.*

9

Gabriel and Anthony began arguing again not fifteen minutes later.

"If you don't stop, I'll knock you off the wagon," said Anthony.

"If you don't stop grumbling, I'll knock *you* out of the wagon!"

"Stop the horse!"

"No!"

"Give me the reins. I'm drawing him up. Can you hear his breathing? He can't go on without a rest!"

"No."

"Gabriel, do as I say!"

"No!"

Barbara could hear a struggle then, grunts and groans and curses as the two men vied for control of Copper. Behind them, the weary horses wheezed and snorted, tugged along by Copper's brisk gait.

"Yes!" said Anthony.

"You imbecile, stop it!" said Gabriel. And then there was a thump and a shout, and Barbara knew that Anthony had been shoved from the wagon seat and onto the road. As they passed him, Anthony called out, "You can't leave me behind, Gabriel! I'll catch this wagon, climb up the back, and cuff you on the head! Just wait!"

Barbara stared at Gemmy. Gemmy stared at Barbara. He couldn't climb into the back, he would find them for certain!

Gabriel shouted, "Giddap, you beast!"

"Wait!" Anthony's voice was not two feet from Barbara as he grappled for the wagon's side. She could hear his frantic breathing. "I shall inform the captain of your behavior; don't think I won't!"

And with a bellow of rage, the man hoisted himself up and over the side and landed on top of the blanket next to Barbara.

Oh, my God! Barbara thought.

But the man didn't seem to notice the difference between one lump and another. He struggled to his feet, shoving aside saddles and hay. Barbara pulled one corner of the blanket from her eye so she could see. Anthony was standing, wobbling, in the wagon, one hand on his pistol, one finger shaking in Gabriel's direction.

"You should not have done that, you traitor! We'll see who is the best soldier!" And he drew his pistol from his side and pointed it at Gabriel.

Barbara shut her eyes tightly. She didn't want to see what was going to happen. She had never seen war, she had only seen arguments between men on the streets of her city. Never had she seen a fight to the death.

But there was no gunfire, and when she looked out again, she saw Anthony with one arm around the neck of Gabriel, struggling to get the reins from his hands. The pistol in his hand waved madly in the air.

"Let go!"

Gabriel gasped, "No!" He bit Anthony's hand but Anthony held tightly. And then, with a quick jerk of his arm, Anthony shoved Gabriel from the wagon. With a squawk, Gabriel hit the road on his side.

Anthony grabbed up the reins and slapped them across Copper's back. "I'm sorry, horse, but to get away from this man we need a bit of speed for a minute. Can you . . . ?"

It was as if Copper understood, and with a whinny and a toss of his sleek head, he lunged into a canter. The horses in the back flattened their ears and nipped at each other as they were forced into a run to keep up. Barbara pulled the blanket back over her head and held her breath.

Little Bit, I hope you are going to be all right! What has this terrible trip done to you?

Gemmy whispered, "Will we stop soon?"

"I think so," Barbara answered.

And from back on the road, she could hear Gabriel's shout, fading as distance was put between him and the wagon. "Come back! I demand you stop now and come back for me!"

But on they ran.

Soon, however, Anthony could be heard saying, "All right there, boy, you've done your duty. Now let's ease up and have a rest. I need a drink, and I think you and your other four-footed friends could use one, too. There's a stream there, see? Sounds refreshing, doesn't it? We can rest until my backside and your hooves feel better. I don't think Gabriel will be able to find us nor reach us in the darkness. We've put too much space between us, and he doesn't know which forks in the road we took."

The wagon slowed and stopped. Barbara held still, waiting. Anthony might care about horses, but she was sure he would care nothing about two girls spying on him from beneath wool blankets and a layer of saddles.

"Ah, there, I'll give each of you a drink of water and loosen the ropes so you can have your heads for a bit of grass. We must save the hay until we reach our camp." The man said nothing else for a while. Barbara and Gemmy looked at each other as they listened to Anthony whistling and walking around, untying horses and leading each one to the stream. Barbara could hear each horse sucking in great gulps of water to cool its throat. She knew it wasn't smart to let a horse have too much water when it was so hot, but there was nothing she could do about it. Slowly, she wiped the beads of sweat from her forehead. How wonderful it would be to smell fresh air again and to feel a breeze on her skin.

At last, Anthony said, "All done there. Now do you not feel better? Have some grass there and ease your hearts. I saw a large blackberry bush back a short ways on the road. They looked so tasty, and I'm very hungry. So you enjoy your grazing, and I will return in just a minute. And then we will be off again."

Gemmy's mouth dropped open in surprise. Barbara knew what she was going to say before she said it. "He's going back up the road a ways! Here's our chance to get away."

Barbara nodded. Gemmy was right. This might be the only opportunity to escape. All they had to do was give Anthony a minute to get out of sight of the wagon, and then they would quietly untie the horses.

"Yes," Barbara whispered. "We'll leave the wagon. I'll get on Little Bit and you can ride behind me. We can lead the other horses back to Philadelphia!"

Gemmy grinned. It was the first time Barbara had seen the girl smile. But then the smile fell away as Gemmy said, "But we don't know the way back. The man said he took many forks in the road. How are we going to know which is the road to the city?"

"We'll worry about that once we get away," said Barbara. "We must take one problem at a time."

The girls held very still and said nothing more

until Anthony's footsteps faded and then could no longer be heard. He was gone.

"Now," said Gemmy. "Let's hurry and we will be free!"

Barbara and Gemmy pushed the blankets off. For a second, Barbara closed her eyes and tipped her head back, her lungs drinking deeply of the sweet, cool summer air. Gemmy tapped her on the back. "What are you waiting for?" As silently as possible, they climbed over the back of the wagon and stretched. Barbara's legs and head ached. But it felt so much better to stand than to be crammed beneath heavy blankets in a jarring wagon.

Barbara hurried back to Little Bit, passing the panting, sweaty horses. The pony had been given enough rope to reach the grass at her feet, and she was eating greedily. Barbara ran her hand down the pony's damp leg, feeling the muscle. *I hope it's nothing serious,* she thought. *I hope she is not permanently lame!* She lifted the leg and looked at the bottom of the hoof. There, wedged in the frog—the soft spot in the center of the foot—was a stone. Barbara flicked the stone free. She hoped this would take care of the limping.

Working at the knot that held the first horse to the wagon, Gemmy threw an exasperated look at

Barbara. "It's too tight!" she said softly. "Have you got a knife?"

Barbara shook her head.

"I can't get the knot loose."

Barbara thought for only a moment. If they couldn't get the horses loose, they would have to take the wagon. Poor Copper would have to pull again. And how would they get past Anthony on the road? If they were riding, they could travel across fields and farms. But in the wagon, the road was the only choice.

"Look," Barbara said suddenly, pointing up the road. There, in the moonlight, she could see the outline of a large barn in a pasture. If they sneaked the horses and wagon into the barn, maybe Anthony would think they'd driven away. They could wait until morning, give the horses a rest, and then go back east.

Gemmy understood. "I'll drive the horse," she said, running to the front and climbing into the seat. She picked up the reins and lowered the wooden brake stick. "You sit in the back of the wagon and watch for that man. We only have a minute. Let's go!"

Barbara gave Little Bit a quick rub on her shoulder, raced to the wagon, and lifted her foot to hop inside.

And then, Barbara felt something cold press between her shoulders. Slowly, she turned her head.

Anthony stood behind her, shaking his head in amused amazement. A glowing lantern hung on one elbow. And in his other hand was a pistol.

It was pointed at Barbara.

10

"Well, well, what have we here?" Anthony asked. "The traitor colonists are pathetic! They send young girls to do their work? I can see we will not have much of a battle if we are fighting children!" He threw back his head and laughed. But the pistol kept its mark.

"Oh," said Barbara. "You don't understand." *What can I say? I have to think of something! Quickly, Barbara, you are a Daughter of Liberty, you are brave and smart and witty. Think of something clever!* "We are only two girls who have lost their way along this dark road tonight. We thought this wagon was abandoned. What luck, we thought! We can drive to the nearest home and tell them of our plight. Tomorrow, in the day's light, we can be reunited with our parents!"

But Anthony lifted the lantern to Barbara's face and sneered. "And girl spies are trained to lie, as well? I know you, Miss Layman. You stole away in the back of this wagon at the request of your traitor parents, to follow us and see where my regiment is located."

"No," said Barbara. "That's not true at all!"

"I am not as dull as you might think," said Anthony.

"It was an accident," Barbara said. "I came down into the stable to get a blanket and fell asleep. I had no idea I would be taken into the countryside."

"Enough!" Anthony shouted. "You girl, at the reins, come down here now if you want your friend to live."

Gemmy climbed from the wagon. Anthony made them both climb into the back of the wagon, and he tied their hands together with twine from the hay bales. Then he shook his finger in their faces. "You will go with me and I will give you to the captain. Spies are hanged, you know. But you are only girls. Perhaps we will only flog you severely and then keep you captive. You could be valuable as hostages."

Barbara said nothing, only staring at Anthony as he talked. She would not let him see how terrified she really was. Gemmy, too, glared at the man silently.

"Fine, then," said Anthony. "You are going to be quiet. That is a good thing. I don't need little girls' chatter." With that, he got into the front of the wagon. He clucked to Copper, but the horse refused to move.

"What is this?" Anthony said. "Giddap, horse, we have to go."

Copper still refused to move.

"I don't want to whip you," said Anthony. "Don't make me do it." He clucked at the horse. But Copper refused to budge.

Anthony lifted the crop from the floorboard and smacked Copper on the rump. Copper bucked but didn't move forward.

"Curses!" said Anthony. He jumped from the seat and grabbed Copper by the cheek straps. "What is the matter with you? Must I put another horse in harness? I don't have the time!" He tried to pull Copper forward, but Copper only rocked back on his rear legs and dug in. He would not move.

"I should shoot you!"

No! thought Barbara. But Anthony unharnessed Copper and led the animal to the rear. He tied him to one of the others.

"Now, which of you will pull for me? Which is the strongest and fastest?" He walked along the row of horses, running his hand along their necks. He stopped at Little Bit. "Ah, yes, you are the smart one, aren't you? Your mistress has told me about you. You are stronger than a horse, she says."

Barbara had to speak then. She couldn't stop the words from coming out. "Leave my pony alone. Leave all the horses alone. You are a thief, and nothing more."

Anthony ignored her. He untied Little Bit and led her to the front of the wagon. The leather straps were tightened around her, and Anthony got into the wagon with the reins. "Move on, there," he said. Little Bit shook her head, and then leaned into the harness. She pulled the wagon back to the center of the road.

"We have to get loose," Gemmy whispered.

"How?" asked Barbara.

"I've gotten free of rope before," said Gemmy. "Do this." She leaned over to Barbara's shoes and slid the twine beneath the metal buckle. Slowly, she began rubbing the ropes back and forth. In just a moment, the twine broke. She showed Barbara her freed wrists. Barbara did the same. The sharp edge of the buckle was as good as a knife.

Gemmy grabbed Barbara's hand and gave it a squeeze. "Now," she whispered. "All we need is a miracle. All we need is some kind of trick."

"Trick!" Barbara said, her voice hushed. "A trick will get us away!" She almost laughed but instead gritted her teeth together so she wouldn't. She didn't want Anthony's attention.

"What?" asked Gemmy, but Barbara held her finger up to keep the girl quiet for a moment. The sound Barbara was going to make needed to be clear and shrill.

Barbara took a very deep breath, pursed her lips together, and watched until Anthony looked up at the sky and wasn't paying close attention to the pony in harness. Then Barbara whistled loud and long.

Little Bit stopped dead in her tracks and reared up. Her front hooves pawed the air and she whined. She jumped back several feet on her hind legs. Anthony was caught off guard. The reins slipped from his hands, and he grabbed to get them back. Barbara whistled again. Again, Little Bit reared and jumped back. The wagon rocked wildly. Anthony stood, reaching for the reins, which had dropped to the road. Little Bit reared again.

Barbara and Gemmy jumped up then and together pushed the off-balance soldier from his seat. He reached for the girls, but his fingers fell short as he tumbled from the wagon and hit the dirt.

"Stop! You can't get away!" he screamed. He leaped to his feet and pulled his pistol from his belt.

Barbara couldn't get the free reins, but it didn't matter. Little Bit knew what to do with the right command. Barbara shouted, "Go!" and Little Bit did just that. The pony took off like a bolt of lightning, galloping as though she had been resting peacefully in her stall all day. From behind, Barbara could hear Anthony shout, and then she heard the crack of gunfire. But the shot went wild. Anthony cursed. "Come back!" He fired again, but missed. The wagon crested a hill and then raced down the other side. Little Bit's ears were up as though she knew this was no trick at all, but a very important mission.

Barbara's Escape

"How are the other horses?" Barbara called to Gemmy.

"They're keeping up!" Gemmy shouted. "But we are going the wrong way. We're going west!"

"We need to get away! Right now it doesn't matter if it's west or east," said Barbara. "Keep watch. When we see a place to hide, we'll get off the road."

Little Bit ran like the wind. Barbara wished she was riding her now, feeling the heart and the power of her pony as she carried her mistress and the kidnapped horses to freedom. *Freedom feels wonderful!* Barbara thought. *No wonder Gemmy ran away. I hope she can always remain free, like we are at this moment!*

And then Gemmy said, "There! Look!" She was pointing to a field on the right side of the road. Surrounding it was a rail fence, and a gate was not far ahead. In the field was a herd of horses. At least fifty grazed in the darkness. Beside a small shed was an old carriage. "Stop here," said Gemmy.

It made no sense to Barbara, but she knew she could trust Gemmy. She called, "Whoa, girl!" and Little Bit slowed to a trot, a walk, and then stopped.

"There is nowhere to hide," Barbara said, turning to the other girl. "There is no barn, no haystack. I don't understand."

"But there are horses," said Gemmy. "Can you find one blade of grass in a field of grass?"

"What do you mean?"

"The soldier is searching for us. He isn't looking at farms now, nor any other horses but those he stole. He is angry and will spend his time looking for us."

Barbara shrugged. "You aren't making sense."

"Looking for us," said Gemmy. "Us. He won't see us if we are blades of grass in a field of grass."

Barbara looked at the horses in the field, at the shed, at the carriage. Then she understood. "Wonderful!" she said. "Let's do it!"

Laughing, Gemmy jumped from the wagon and opened the gate to the field. Barbara steered Little Bit through and up to the shed. She maneuvered Little Bit back and forth until the wagon was next to the carriage that was parked outside the shed. Climbing from the wagon seat, she unharnessed Little Bit and gave the pony a pat on the rump to encourage her to join the grazing horses.

"Before we let the others go," said Gemmy, "we

must look at them carefully so we will know them again in the morning."

"Yes," said Barbara. As she and Gemmy untied each horse, they looked at the height, the length of mane and tail, the markings. Then they clapped their hands to get them to join the herd.

But the last horse to let loose, the one immediately behind the wagon, still had a knot too tight to untie.

"How shall we cut this?" asked Barbara.

Gemmy went to the shed, rummaged around, and came out smiling. In her hand was a sickle, a long curved blade used to cut tall weeds. "This isn't a knife, but then neither is a shoe buckle!" With several quick sawing motions, the rope came off the back of the wagon.

"Run, my friend!" Gemmy said to the horse. With a whinny and a buck, the horse darted off and joined the others.

To the east, the sky was beginning to grow light. A pink glow hovered over the treetops, chasing the stars away and draining the moon of its bright glow.

Gemmy smiled. "The horses are resting now, and we should, too. We can hide in the shed and get some sleep. The soldier may keep looking, but he won't see us. Our horses will be right in front of his face, but he'll keep on walking, watching for a wrecked wagon, two exhausted girls, and seven spent horses."

Barbara nodded. She was suddenly aware of the weariness in her bones. She and Gemmy went into the shed, found some musty straw, and fluffed it into a tolerable mattress. As they lay down, Gemmy said, "I'm glad to have known you, Barbara. I will miss you when I leave."

Her mouth could barely move as sleep wrapped her in its soft arms, but Barbara said, "Leave? Where are you going?"

"Away," said Gemmy. "I must keep running."

"No, you don't have to run," Barbara said. "No, you don't." Her eyes would no longer open, and she could feel the straw begin to spin slowly beneath her. "No, you don't," she murmured again. Or maybe it was only her thoughts. "You must stay with me. You are a brave Daughter of Liberty. You mustn't go."

11

It was the sound of birds that brought Barbara back to consciousness. Chattering blue jays and starlings were on the roof of the shed, arguing over who had the right to sit there. Barbara sat up and ran her hand over her face, brushing sleep and straw dust from her cheeks and eyes. How long had she slept? What time was it?

Then she realized she was still in the shed in the field of horses. Anthony had not found them! Gemmy's idea had worked!

"Gemmy!" she said, turning to look at the spot where the girl had slept. "You were right, we . . ."

But Gemmy was gone. Only an impression in

the straw was there, the place where Barbara's new friend had slept.

Barbara stood up. "Gemmy! Where are you? You can't be gone! I want you to come home with me!" She ran to the shed's door and looked out. "Gemmy! Come back!"

The sun was directly above. It was noon already. And the horses continued to graze, stomp their hooves and swish their tails, and nip at each other if they got too close.

Barbara walked to the wagon and put her hand on the side. She shaded her eyes with the other hand. "Gemmy!"

She could see no one. Only the sea of horses.

Oh, Gemmy, I didn't want you to run away. I think my parents would let you live with us. But you didn't give me the chance to ask them. What are you going to do? Will you be safe?

Then she saw Little Bit coming her way. And Gemmy was leading her.

"Gemmy!" Barbara said. "I thought you'd gone!"

Gemmy shook her head. "I wouldn't leave before I helped you gather your horses together for the return trip. They have rested well. Only one seems to still have tender feet. I think in the daylight, you shall travel with little problem. Just keep your eyes ahead, don't stop to speak to anyone, and look as though you know exactly what you're doing."

"That's good advice," said Barbara. She helped Gemmy collect the other horses and tie them to the wagon. Then she hitched Little Bit to the harness. Copper was a handful, too anxious and headstrong for Barbara to control if he pulled the wagon. Little Bit would make the excursion easier. *Oh, I'll be so glad to be home,* she thought as she climbed into the seat and picked up the reins. *My mother and father are surely frantic by now, wondering where I've gone. I'll be as glad to see them as they will be to see me.*

Barbara looked down at Gemmy, standing in the grass with her hands in the pockets of her skirt.

"Come with me," said Barbara.

"I have to go on," said Gemmy.

"Why?"

"Until I can find a place to be safe and free, I must keep running."

"But you can stay with us."

Gemmy shook her head. "Your parents don't

want a runaway slave in their home. I would be a burden."

Barbara thought for a moment. "But you can get a job at the tavern. There is a vacant position. The Blacks would hire you, I know it. Look at all you've done to help me, to help them. You've rescued the horses that belong to their guests. They will be grateful."

Gemmy hesitated. "A job?"

Barbara nodded. She couldn't believe it, but she was telling a lie. There were no jobs at Black's Tavern. If there were, Mrs. Layman would be given the position, since she had lost her work at Boxler's Milliner. But somehow, this lie seemed all right. If it got Gemmy to come home with her and meet the family, the lie was not so bad. "A job, and no one will ever tell where you came from. It will be a secret that not even a British soldier can draw from our lips."

"A job," Gemmy said again. "To make money? I will make money and be able to live like a true, free black girl?"

Barbara nodded.

Gemmy crossed her arms. She stared at her bare toes for a very long moment. And then she hopped onto the wagon seat by Barbara. She laughed openly. "Yes, then, I'll be pleased to ride into Philadelphia with you, Barbara Layman. Let's go!"

Barbara only needed to ask two farmers' wives, strolling along the road with their milk cows, for directions to the city. "Just keep on this road until you reach a crossroads, then go left," one woman said. "That is the road to Philadelphia."

"Thank you!" Barbara said, and Little Bit, who seemed to understand that they would be home again soon, picked up her ears and her trot.

The sun was low to their backs as they came into the city and followed the many streets to Mulberry. Men, women, and children paused to stare at them openly as they passed.

We must be a dreadful, curious sight, Barbara thought. *We are filthy and can barely sit upright because of fatigue. The horses behind us are caked with dirt and foam. Our wagon wheels are wobbling and could come off at any moment. I'd be worried if I wasn't so tired!* She laughed at this, which seemed to make the curious onlookers even more dubious. *A good bath and good sleep and they would not recognize us. They would see what fine ladies are hiding beneath this dirt.*

Barbara steered Little Bit into the alley, and they rattled to the Black's Tavern stable. Before they had reached the paddock fence, Mrs. Layman was at the wagon, screaming with joy and pulling her daughter from the seat and into her arms. "You're home! You're safe! Oh, thank God! You're safe!"

12

Barbara and Gemmy were invited into the tavern to sit in the Red Horse Room with the Black and Layman families to tell the story of their adventure. Barbara, in clean clothes and stockings, was tired, yet found she couldn't stop talking. It was as if her mouth alone had more energy than her entire body. She told the tale of the noises she'd heard from upstairs, of the men with their lanterns and whispers in the stable, and of having to hide beneath the blanket so she wouldn't be discovered.

Patsy's eyes grew wide as Barbara spoke. *Yes,* Barbara thought. *This was truly a Daughter of Liberty adventure!*

As she told about the thieves and the pistol and

the twine and the herd of horses on the hillside, no one said a word. Mr. Black and Mr. Layman rubbed their chins and took in the details. Soon, Barbara knew, they would get word out to their friends in the city, warning them of the thieves so they could be cautious and on the lookout. Patsy sat on the edge of her chair, hands fidgeting in her lap, looking as though she were almost envious of the excitement Barbara had seen.

Gemmy, however, sat slumped in her chair, staring at the floor, clearly feeling awkward with the attention.

At last the saga was done. Barbara took a deep breath and let it out. "That's it," she said. Her throat was sore from so much talking. "And I wouldn't have made it back if it hadn't been for Gemmy."

"Gemmy," said Mrs. Layman, extending her hand to the runaway slave. Gemmy took it awkwardly, then let it drop. "I don't believe we've met properly. How is it you were in the wagon with Barbara? She didn't tell us that."

Gemmy looked stricken. She glanced at Barbara and then back at the floor.

But Barbara said, "Please, Mother, may we talk more tomorrow? I can barely think straight. I need to sleep."

Barbara's Escape

"Of course," said Mrs. Layman. "Poor dears, you've had a day I can't even imagine. Paul, we ladies will leave you gentlemen to your duties."

Mr. Black and Mr. Layman bowed as the women and girls left the room. With Barbara leaning on her mother's arm and Mrs. Black holding Gemmy's, they went outside to the backyard. Patsy followed quietly. Crickets were already beginning to chirp in the flowers along the walk. Evening was on its way.

Katherine waved from the kitchen. "Hello, girls! Word has spread quickly. Nicholas told me that you are heroes!"

Barbara shook her head. "Not heroes," she said.

"Oh, yes," said Katherine. "It's a shame the Andersons aren't here anymore. They would have been proud of you, too, Barbara."

"Oh," said Mrs. Layman. "Where are the Quaker ladies? I didn't know they had left, Rebecca. When did this happen?"

"This morning," explained Mrs. Black. "You were too distressed with Barbara's absence; I didn't see the need to bring up any other matters at the time. But now that Barbara is here and well, praise God, I will tell you that the sisters found employment in the home of a wealthy man and his wife. The home is not far from where the Andersons' parents live, and they decided it would be best to take that position as their mother and father are ailing. I will miss them, but I realize they did what they needed to do."

Mrs. Layman said, "I see. I will miss them, too." Then she said, "Would you, perhaps, be looking to fill the jobs they have left?"

Mrs. Black put one arm around Barbara and the other around Mrs. Layman. Gemmy stepped back several steps and looked away as if uncomfortable with the closeness. "I was going to ask if you would like to help us out now," said Mrs. Black. "We do need the extra hands. It will be very busy, with both of the Quaker ladies gone now, but perhaps I will be able to find someone to fill the other position soon."

"But I know who can take the second position!" said Barbara. "I know someone who is trustworthy and smart and strong and eager. Someone who needs the work and likes our families very much."

"Oh?" asked Mrs. Black. "And who might that be?"

Barbara pointed at Gemmy. Gemmy stared at Barbara, then at Mrs. Black. Her mouth opened, but no words came out.

"Hmmm," said Mrs. Black. "Is this true, Gemmy? Are you looking for employment?"

After a long moment, Gemmy said, "Oh, well, yes, ma'am, I am."

"And are you trustworthy, smart, strong, and eager?"

"I suppose I am. Yes, ma'am, I am."

Mrs. Black put her hand on Gemmy's shoulder. "Do you like our families very much?"

Gemmy broke into a smile. "Of course I do. You've been kind to me."

"It's settled, then," said Mrs. Black with a clap of her hands. "I have my replacements. Della and Gemmy, can you begin in the morning, after the excitement has calmed and we've all rested?"

"Yes," said Mrs. Layman.

"Oh, yes," said Gemmy.

That night, Mr. Layman cleaned the tack room and made a comfortable place for Gemmy to stay. He provided a mattress, a small table and wash-bowl, and some towels. "This is the best I can do," he said. "I hope you will find it suitable."

"It's wonderful," said Gemmy softly.

Mrs. Layman and Barbara stood at the tack room door. "Is there anything else you need?" asked Mrs. Layman.

"Oh, no, ma'am. This is just fine."

"We have our morning meal at six," Mr. Layman said. "Barbara will wake you if you'd care to join us," Mr. Layman said.

"That would be fine," said Gemmy. "And thank you for everything."

"Good night," said Mr. and Mrs. Layman.

"Good night," said Barbara.

"God bless you all," said Gemmy. "And good night."

As Barbara curled up to sleep after the kisses of her father and mother, her father said, "One last thing, daughter. Mr. Ford came by the tavern this evening to bring some candlesticks to Mrs. Black. He heard of your bravery in saving the horses. He said such a girl deserves a gift."

"Oh?" asked Barbara.

"Yes," said her father. "He said that as soon as Dark Star is old enough, he is yours."

Barbara said, "Really? I shall have that beautiful colt?"

"Indeed," said Mr. Layman. "Now sleep, my girl. Sleep."

And Barbara did. And she dreamed of horses and fields and sunlight and peace.

About the Author

Besides writing for young people and adults, Elizabeth Massie loves traveling and seeing new sights. "I love taking roads I've never been on before and seeing new towns, forests, houses, and people. To write stories, you should enjoy learning and exploring. And to write about people, it's important to care about them and to be interested in them. Remember, everyone's life is a story." She and her sister, Barbara Spilman Lawson, are presently working on new book projects together.

DAUGHTERS *of* LIBERTY

<u>INDEPENDENCE DAY 1776</u>

It all started with the Daughters of Liberty
and their adventures in Philadelphia....

PATSY'S DISCOVERY

PATSY AND THE DECLARATION

BARBARA'S ESCAPE

By Elizabeth Massie

A MINSTREL BOOK

Published by Pocket Books

1337-02

𝔍n her hometown of Luck, Wisconsin, in 1908 Madeline "Moe" McDonohugh is convinced excitement and adventure are right under her nose!

Heartland Series

Come Away with Me 53716-4/$3.99

Take to the Sky 53717-2/$3.99

Luck Follows Me 53718-0/$3.99

By Laurie Lawlor
Illustrated by Jane Kendall

 A MINSTREL® BOOK

Published by Pocket Books